THE KEEPERS
OF TIME

Russell F. Moran

Coddington Press
The Keepers of Time

Copyright © 2017 by Russell F. Moran
Printed in the United States of America

ISBN: 0996346678
ISBN: 9780996346672
Cover Design by Erin Kelly
http://erinkelly.webs.com/

www.morancom.com

DEDICATION

This book is dedicated to the men and women of the United States Navy.

ACKNOWLEDGEMENTS

A writer does his work behind a closed door, but no work comes to daylight without the input from many people. As always, I thank my wife, Lynda, for her attentive reading and re-reading of my many drafts, and for laughing at my jokes. I also thank my eagle-eyed friend, John White, for his proofreading and editing.

My special thanks to Dennis Ciano, retired NYPD homicide detective. Dennis has worked extensively as a police procedures consultant to numerous TV shows, including *The Black List, Unforgettable,* and *Elementary,* as well as a major motion picture and an HBO original series.

AUTHOR'S NOTE

You will find a **Cast of Characters** after the last chapter of the book. It can be frustrating to come across a character on page 150, who you first met on page 20, especially if you've put the book down for a few days. I've seen this done in Russian literature, and I happily add a cast of characters to *The Keepers of Time,* as well as my other novels.

CHAPTER ONE

Something's wrong.
What's going on?
This isn't right.
Where the hell are we?

⇥ ⇤

On June 1, 2017, the day after Memorial Day, Carrier Strike Group 2311 departed New York Harbor and the festivities of Fleet Week. We paraded under the Verrazano Bridge, led by our cruiser and trailed by our two frigates. We set course for Boston to pick up parts for our planes before we headed for the Persian Gulf. The group steamed east with Long Island on our port side.

Jack stood next to me on the open air section of the flag bridge. It was a beautiful June morning, with a temperature of 74 degrees and a cloudless sky. I had received permission from the Navy Department for my husband, Naval Reserve Lieutenant Jack Thurber, to accompany me on our cruise. As an admiral and the

1

Commanding Officer of Carrier Strike Group 2311 I had clout, but it still took some doing.

At 8:45 a.m. we steamed off Long Island's Hamptons and its beautiful waterfront mansions, a pleasant way to start a long deployment. Bright sunlight, perfect temperature, beautiful scenery, and Jack standing next to me. I felt great.

Suddenly, everything turned dark.

⟫⊱ ⊰⟪

Thousands of sailors shouted at the same time. The beautiful June morning suddenly changed to pitch black. No moon, no stars, no lights ashore. The temperature felt like it dropped 10 degrees, as if we just steamed into a large closet with the lights off.

The intercom sounded.

"Admiral Patterson, this is Captain Tomlinson on the bridge. We're going to general quarters, ma'am."

"Very well, captain, I concur."

The ear shattering sound of an electronic bell pierced the darkness, accompanied by the officer of the deck yelling,

"General quarters, general quarters, all hands man your battle stations. This is not a drill. I repeat, this is not a drill."

⟫⊱ ⊰⟪

"Jack, what the fuck just happened?"

I try to avoid profanity, including when I speak to Jack. It's unprofessional, vulgar, and doesn't properly communicate a thought. But "what the fuck" was the only phrase I could come up with. Jack looked at his watch and turned on its backlight.

"I'm guessing we have about another minute before daylight comes back," said Jack.

"Oh shit," I said. My anti-profanity rule wasn't doing well.

2

"Jack, you don't think for a minute…"

"Yes, I do, Ashley, and we only have about a minute left," said Jack.

The darkness suddenly returned to bright daylight and the warmth returned to the air. Everyone on deck put a hand over his eyes because of the sudden glare.

"This didn't happen, did it Jack? Please tell me this didn't happen."

"Look at the beautiful mansions, babe," said Jack. "They're gone. And where's our cruiser and frigates? They're gone too."

"Jack, you don't think we hit a…"

"Yes, I think we did, hon. We hit a wormhole."

"And it feels like we're aground," I said.

※ ※

"Captain Tomlinson, this is Admiral Patterson. Lieutenant Thurber and I are coming to the bridge."

Jack and I entered the bridge. The quartermaster of the watch shouted, "Attention on deck."

"As you were," I said.

Captain Tomlinson was standing next to the navigator.

"What's our depth, Joe?" Tomlinson said to the navigator.

"According to our chart we should have 150 feet of water under us, but sonar shows *zero.*"

"Engage the port-side bow and stern thrusters," Tomlinson said to the officer of the deck.

We could feel the ship edging ever so slightly to starboard. Tomlinson repeated the maneuver every 30 seconds, not wanting to overtax the thruster engines.

"What's our depth now?"

"Sonar shows 100 feet under us, captain."

"Thank God we were near the edge of the slope. Let's get a bit further out and then I'll try to maneuver," Tomlinson said.

"I'm now showing 150 feet under us, captain," the OOD said.

"Right 20 degrees rudder, all ahead one-third," the captain said. "Keep your eye on that sonar screen."

The *Reagan* surged forward, now in deep water. Jack and I walked over to Tomlinson.

"Admiral, I've never seen anything like this before. Our chart showed deep water, but we were almost hard aground."

"What's the tide, captain?" I said.

"Almost full high tide, ma'am. I'm stumped. We almost went hard aground in what our chart showed was 150 feet of water."

Harry Tomlinson is a serious professional, and I was happy to serve with him. He's a tall guy, about 6'3" with short-cropped brown hair. He keeps in shape with a regular exercise routine. But something about Captain Harry didn't look right.

"Harry, you look like hell," I said, softly so as not to draw attention. "Are you feeling okay?"

"I'm fine, admiral," he said, his eyes almost closed. His face was pale as snow.

I've known Harry Tomlinson for years. The guy simply didn't look well. Going aground can ruin a captain's day, and Harry looked like he was still aground.

"I want you to go to sick bay to get checked out," I said.

"Please, admiral, I'm fine. Let's talk about the crazy thing that just happened to us."

"Harry, that's a direct order. On second thought, stay put. I'm calling the medical officer to come to the bridge."

I looked at Jack, who had already picked up a phone and said "This is Lieutenant Thurber, get me the medical officer."

The ship's medical officer, Commander George Molloy, entered the bridge followed by two corpsman with a stretcher.

Molloy took Tomlinson's pulse and blood pressure, and gave him a quick going over.

"Captain," Molloy said, "I'm recommending we get you to sick bay immediately. It looks like you've had a cardiac event and I want you off your feet and on the stretcher."

Harry looked too weak to argue. The corpsmen lifted him onto the stretcher and carried him off the bridge.

"I want regular reports on the captain's condition, commander."

"Aye aye, admiral," Molloy said. Then he leaned over to my ear. "I'll be honest with you, ma'am, he doesn't look good."

⊶⊷

I ordered Commander Mike Blakely, the executive officer, to gather all department heads for a meeting in the wardroom. The wardroom is the place on a Navy ship where the officers eat. It's also a regular meeting space. At 30 feet by 25 feet, it was a fairly large room, with dining tables in the middle that can be put together to make a conference table.

"Ladies and gentlemen, attention to Admiral Patterson," Blakely said.

Present at the meeting was Lieutenant Commander Jane Bollard, the communications officer, Lieutenant Bill Cummings, the ship's deck officer, Commander Lysle Phillips, commander of the air wing, Commander Muriel Parker, engineering officer, and Commander Joseph Johnston, the navigator. Also with us was Major Tucker Clark, commander of the attached Marine contingent, and Max Baxter, my chief of staff. Lieutenant Jack, my husband and deputy chief of staff, sat next to me. I stood in front of the group.

"I just spoke to the medical officer in sick bay," I said. "Captain Tomlinson is in stable condition. His vitals are okay and he's conscious and alert. Hopefully he dodged a bullet."

I looked at Father Rick Sampson, the ship's chaplain, and put a "please fill us in" look on my face.

"I just came from sick bay," Father Rick said, "and I can report that Captain Tomlinson is doing as well as can be expected under the circumstances. I request that you all keep him in your prayers."

"Okay, let's get to the matter at hand," I said. "Folks, I'm going to tell you what I know. We all saw what happened a half hour ago. Daylight became darkness, and then shortly returned to daylight. I've experienced this before, and so has Lieutenant Jack and Father Rick. Based on what our eyes told us, the disappearance of all of the buildings ashore, and the sudden vanishing of the rest of our strike group, I'm about to tell you all something you're gonna have a hard time believing. We've traveled through time."

I let my last words sink in.

"That odd light and dark phenomenon we experienced is a phenomenon known as a wormhole," I said, "also known as a time portal. We are no longer in the year 2017, and God knows what year we're really in. You all look skeptical, and that's fine by me. If you simply accepted what I just said, I'd assume you're all lunatics, and I know that you're anything but."

My last comment brought a few laughs, which is what I intended. Since I just took command of Carrier Strike Group 2311, it's one of my responsibilities to get to know the senior officers on my flagship. And because the captain is in sick bay, it looks like I'm in command of this ship as well. I started this cruise with four ships under my command. Now we're down to just the *Reagan.*

"I've given you a brief summary of what happened," I said. "Now I want to hear any and all questions, as well as comments."

Lt. Commander Jane Bollard, our communications officer, raised her hand.

"With all due respect, admiral, you just said that we've traveled through time. Pardon me, but my parents raised a realist. I'm at a loss to grasp what you just said."

"Commander, in answer to your question," I said, "allow me to pose a question that may bring things into focus. Please tell us about our ship's communications abilities."

"Well that has me stumped, admiral," Bollard said. "We don't seem to have ship-to-shore capabilities, although we're not sure that there's anyone ashore to communicate with. If there are people ashore, they sure as hell aren't answering our calls. We're not getting communications from our usual sources, including Naval Operations in Washington. Also, we're getting no weather reports at all. It's as if this ship is alone at sea. But the most startling thing is that we've lost all Internet access, including, obviously, email. I'll let Commander Johnston, the navigator, comment on our GPS and satellite status."

"We've lost all GPS capabilities," said Commander Johnston. "It's like our satellites have simply disappeared. Tonight we expect a cloudless sky, based on this morning's last weather report, so I'm going to get a good celestial position. I'm sure the stars are still there. If I may, admiral, you said that you, Lieutenant Thurber, and Father Rick have experienced this phenomenon before. Could you please explain that to us? All we seem to know is that we're alone at sea, and we don't know why."

I knew this was coming, and I welcomed it. These smart people are understandably freaked out over this thing called time travel (*as if I'm not!*) I had to bring them up to date, whatever the hell date this is.

"Folks, Commander Johnston just hit it on the head," I said. "You would all like to know what I know, and what Lieutenant Thurber and Father Rick know, about this weird phenomenon. I'll start by telling you how Jack—I have a hard time calling my husband lieutenant so bear with me—Jack and I met in April of 1861."

I shut up and let those words sink in. I learned over the years that a great way to grab the attention of an audience is to hit them with something crazy, something from out of left field, so I just did.

"I'm sure I heard that wrong, admiral," Commander Muriel Parker said, "Did you say that you and Lieutenant Thurber met in 1861?"

"That's correct, Muriel, and I won't dance around the point. Father Rick was with us when we met. You're about to learn how the three of us traveled through time. Let me just begin with a question. "Have any of you heard of *The Gray Ship* incident?"

"Yes, admiral," said Commander Lysle Phillips, the air wing commander. "I read all about it a few years ago, but like most people I just assumed it was a confused story from a crew that became lost at sea, no disrespect intended, ma'am."

"Well, the story is true, and Jack and I lived through it, as well as Father Rick. I was the commanding officer of the *USS California* in April 2013. While on our way to Charleston, South Carolina, the ship hit a strange turbulence at night, and suddenly the dark sky became light, similar to what just happened to us on the *Reagan*. And just like we experienced a half-hour ago, the event lasted for only two minutes. After shore surveillance we determined that we had gone from 2013 to 1861. The turbulence that we hit was a wormhole, a time portal in the sea. I soon discovered that Jack Thurber, a crew member, had not only experienced time travel himself, but he had written a bestselling book on the subject, *Living History— Stories of Time Travel Through the Ages*. In what became known as *The Gray Ship* incident, the entire crew of the *California* spent four months in the Civil War. When we managed to find the wormhole and return to 2013, we found a world that had changed, not completely, but it was different from the one we left. Oh, yes, I should mention, when we returned we found out that we were gone from the year 2013 for only seven hours, not four months."

"Admiral, I've read about that *Gray Ship* incident as well," said Joe Johnston, the navigator. "If I recall, you found the wormhole and returned to 2013 by steaming around the ocean for a couple of weeks before you hit it. But I have a big concern. As you know ma'am, this morning we damn near went aground—at high tide— in 150 feet of water, according to our chart. But, of course, sonar showed zero. We have a reliable fix, or at least I think it's reliable, but if we try to cross over that coordinate, we'll go aground."

"You nailed the problem, Joe," I said. "If we've learned anything about time travel in the past few years, it's this: To get back, go to the spot where you came from. But where we came from isn't navigable. I'm not going to gild the lily for you folks. This could be a *big* problem."

"Admiral," said Commander Mike Blakely, the Executive Officer, "could you share with us our immediate plans?"

"Yes, Mike," I said. "This ship is the property of the United States Navy, and even though we don't have a useable set of orders, our job is to do whatever we can to further our national defense. And right now, that means trying to figure out what year we're in so we can report back when (*When? How about if?*) we return. We know that we were steaming off what we knew to be Eastern Long Island when we hit the wormhole. For openers, we're going to head back to New York City."

CHAPTER TWO

Two Months Earlier

Jack and I sat in our favorite diner in Norfolk, Virginia. Ever since we got married four years ago, we have breakfast together, a great way to start the day with the one you love. But this morning, Jack seemed upset about something.

"Ashley, you're not going to take another carrier strike group command, are you?"

"Jack, honey, I follow orders. It's part of the deal with being in the Navy. They tell me what to do and I do it. This assignment will give me a pick of commands in the future. I better take it. Carrier Strike Group 2311 is a plumb job. Hey, why the pickle puss?"

"Maybe this sounds like I'm being over-protective, babe," said Jack, "but I'm worried about you. You're only 39 years old, the youngest vice admiral in the Navy, and I think you're taking on too much work. I see it in your face. You're under too much damn stress."

I looked around. The café was almost empty except for an elderly couple at the far end of the room. I got up and slid into Jack's side of the booth. I leaned over and kissed him. He was wearing my favorite cologne, a scent that drives me crazy. I looked into his eyes, his deep blue eyes. This is nuts, I thought, two grownups sitting in a diner acting like a couple of teenagers. But that's the way it is with Jack and me. We don't just have a marriage, but a relationship that seems to get closer as the years go by. We love each other, we like each other, and we think of each other as best friends, not just spouses. I felt the same way he did about my going on an extended deployment. But as the Navy's youngest vice admiral, I couldn't and shouldn't turn down the job. The fact that I'm a woman and African-American gives me an extra sense of responsibility. Yes, commanding a carrier strike group is a job—a big one. I rested my hand on Jack's leg as we looked into each other's eyes.

"Jack, sometimes I think that my life works better when I'm under stress. I hate the idea of being away from you for a long time, but I look at it this way; after this command, things will quiet down in my career. I love my Navy, but you're right. Sea duty can be a pain in the ass. I've been politicking like crazy to become superintendent of Annapolis. Wouldn't that be great? I'd go to work and come home. We'd be able to have a normal life together. My good friend, Senator Max Fisher, as you know, is the new head of the Senate Armed Forces Committee. Max told me that I've got a good shot at the Academy job, especially with a carrier strike group command on my resume."

"Hey, honey," said Jack, "I'm being stupid. When we got married I knew you had a traveling job. Hell, we even met at sea. You know how I feel about you. When you're away I feel like I'm adrift, to use a nautical term."

"Jack, are you upset because you gave up your job as editor-in-chief at *The Washington Times?*"

"Maybe that's part of it, Ashley, but I really hated the job. I'd rather be reporting and writing, which is what I do best. But now, maybe I have too much time on my hands."

"Too much time on your hands?" I said. "Hey, Jack, your latest book just hit number one on *The New York Times* Best Seller List. Didn't you tell me that your agent said he thinks you have a clear shot at a National Book Award? I mean holy shit, Jack, you've already won a Pulitzer Prize, and now you're a famous author. I noticed in the Book Review section last week that in the past five years there has only been *one week* when none of your books was on the best seller list. When I'm underway and want to see you, all I have to do is turn the TV to a talk show to catch your handsome puss."

We kissed. I thought about what a sight we must be. An admiral making out with a handsome guy in a booth in a diner.

"I've had a successful career in the Navy so far, Jack—just ask my parents, who never shut up about it. But until four years ago I felt there was something missing in my life. Then I discovered what was missing—you."

As a consistent best-selling author, Jack makes a ton of money from his book royalties alone, which is supplemented by magazine article fees and his constant TV appearances. After he gave up his job as Editor-in-Chief of *The Washington Times,* he formed his own publishing company. Jack is handsome—crazy handsome, and he attracts a lot of young women to shows he appears on, something that his agent loves. I make a good salary as a vice admiral, but Jack's income has made us wealthy.

Jack has a rare talent with the written word. He mainly writes non-fiction, but recently he's been spinning out novels, and the public seems to love them as much as his non-fiction works. His most recent novel is *Rawhide – A Manhattan Western,* a hysterically funny book about life on Seventh Avenue, New York City's Garment District. It's loaded with crazy characters who can't seem to get things right. As always, I was his first-round editor. I think Jack is trying to groom me for a second career after I retire from the Navy.

When Jack and I met, I was a widow. I lost my husband Felix, a Marine major, to combat in Afghanistan. Jack was a widower, his wife having died in a horrible car accident. Jack actually came upon the aftermath of accident, and her body. Jack and I were both lonely, about the same age, and wildly attracted to each other, even though I was the captain of his ship and he was a junior officer. More about that later.

Jack now holds the rank of lieutenant. He should be promoted to lieutenant commander as soon as he has the necessary time in service. And it's not just a ceremonial title. Jack isn't just a civilian in a military uniform, he's a serious naval officer, and he taught himself. Jack takes on everything he tackles with a dedication that inspires me. When I assume a new command, I can count on Jack, Mr. Encyclopedia Brain, to help bring me up to speed. Just the other day, he gave me a one-hour rundown on every aspect of Carrier Strike Group 2311, without even looking at his notes. Jack's my most trusted advisor.

"Hey, Jack. I just got a great idea. The strike group is due to visit Manhattan in two months for Fleet Week, right after I take command. Then we deploy to the Persian Gulf for six months. Why don't you write a feature article about the impact of a long deployment on sailors' lives? It would be great. I bet one of the major papers or magazines would pick it up in a heartbeat. Hell, you're still a reserve officer, so you will just have some active duty time. And we can be together."

"Wouldn't the Navy get a bit concerned about an admiral taking her husband aboard on a long deployment?"

"No problem, Jack. In the modern Navy it's kind of rare, but not unheard of. I'm sure I can clear this through Naval Operations. (Well, I was *pretty sure*). You'll love it, interviewing sailors and officers on all of the ships in the group. And you'll produce another great article, maybe even a book. I think it would be great for morale to have a famous author aboard my flagship."

"And where would I stay aboard ship?"

"My stateroom is pretty big. We'd have to exercise discretion, of course," I said as I winked at him. "And we can't be too loud when we make love," I whispered.

Jack smiled and grabbed my hand.

"Hey, Jack, let's do this."

"Aye aye, sweetheart."

Getting clearance for Jack to join our cruise would take some persuading with NavOps. I really didn't expect much difficulty. For an admiral's spouse to join her on a cruise is a bit out of the ordinary, to say the least. But Jack has a lot of credibility in the world of the Navy. He's written extensively on naval subjects, and the senior brass loves him. I'm convinced that my idea of his writing a feature article, maybe even a book, on the impact of naval deployments on ships' personnel is a good one. Besides all that, I love being with Jack. We have what I think is a kind of rare relationship. We've been married over four years, but are still as love-struck as the day we met. I felt a little guilty about my plan to get Jack stationed aboard my flagship. A little guilty, but not that much. What the hell, why have a high rank if you can't use it now and then?

Jack has a natural grace around people, and my crew will get over the fact that he's my husband. I'm going to appoint him as my aide, my deputy chief of staff. Commander Max Baxter, my chief of staff, is a good guy. I think he'll get along great with Jack, and, because of Jack's diplomatic skills, Max won't feel pushed aside. Everything will go smoothly.

I think.

CHAPTER THREE

I took command of Carrier Strike Group 2311 at the end of April 2017. A carrier strike group consists of surface ships, including an aircraft carrier, a guided missile cruiser, and at least two frigates or large destroyers. It used to be called a carrier battle group. My flagship, the carrier I'll be aboard, is the *USS Ronald Reagan*, named after my favorite president. The cruiser was the *USS Bunker Hill*, a *Ticonderoga* class missile cruiser. Our frigates were the *USS Samuel B. Roberts* and the *USS Stark*.

The *USS Ronald Reagan* (CVN-76) is a Nimitz Class carrier, christened in 2001. She was the first ship to be named for a still-living ex-president. *The Gipper*, as some people affectionately call her, is big, 1092 feet in length with a beam of 134 feet at the waterline, and 252 feet at the flight deck level. We carry 3,200 people in the ship's company and 2,480 in the air wing. As a nuclear powered carrier, the *Reagan* can steam uninterrupted for as long as 25 years. Imagine 25 years without a refill? When I'm driving, I always find stopping for fuel to be a pain in the ass, so the *Reagan*'s cruising range suited me just fine.

NavOps approved Jack's assignment to the *Reagan* for our Persian Gulf deployment. A command as big and complicated as a carrier strike group can be unnerving, and my nerves were letting me know that. But having my Jack aboard helped settle my stomach. Every morning since I took command, Jack reviewed various parts of the strike group with me. His memory for detail is amazing. It's like having an aircraft carrier user's manual next to you.

I'd be lying to you if I said I wasn't intimidated as I walked up to the *Reagan*. I'm in charge of this gigantic ship as well as three others, as my jumpy stomach pointed out to me. I looked up at the *Reagan*'s flight deck towering above me and I felt overwhelmed. Truth is I was scared shitless. Having Jack aboard helped to calm me down. He's a guy who I can level with and reveal what's really going on inside my head, not my admiral's head, *my* head.

The shrill sound of the bosun's pipe sounded throughout the ship. "Carrier Strike Group 2311, arriving." This is the traditional Navy of announcing the arrival of a dignitary, including an admiral or the ship's captain. I walked up the gangplank, saluted the colors on the stern, and then returned the salute from the officer of the deck as I entered the quarterdeck. The quarterdeck gets its name from the raised platform behind the main mast on sailing ships. In the modern Navy it's the ceremonial area of a ship, sort of like a welcoming lobby.

I proceeded to "admiral's country," the Navy's quaint name for the area of a ship where an embarked admiral hangs out.

Jack was waiting for me in my office. As planned, we reviewed the personnel records to see if we knew any of the people aboard.

"Oh my God, Jack, Father Rick Sampson has come out of retirement for this cruise. He's gonna be the *Reagan*'s chaplain."

Father Rick Sampson is a special friend of ours. He officiated at our marriage four years ago. Fr. Rick was also aboard the *California* during our weird *Gray Ship* incident when we traveled through time back to the Civil War. Yes, I know, more about that later. He's a great guy to have aboard, and the crews always love him. Fr. Rick is a tall, broad-shouldered man, and a bit portly. He has a wonderful sense of humor that never lets up. He doesn't so much laugh as explode with laughter. He's also a great advisor. Father Rick loves history as much as Jack, and he helps me keep things in perspective.

Fleet Week, an annual event held in New York City, is a hell of a lot of fun. This year it's scheduled to begin on May 25 and end on May 31. The highlights of the week were Navy and Coast Guard ships, along with their crews. The ships are tied up to piers or anchored all around New York City. Because of our size and the depth of water we draw, the *USS Ronald Reagan* was anchored off Staten Island. The rest of the group tied up to piers at various locations in the city. Altogether, our strike group was just shy of 7,000 sailors, all looking forward to a few days in the Big Apple.

Nine ships, including all four from Carrier Strike Group 2311, began the Parade of Ships, one of the highlights of Fleet Week. We passed under the Verrazano Bridge and continued up the Hudson to the George Washington Bridge where we would turn around. Events like Fleet Week bring out a healthy patriotism among the visitors, which I love. As we sailed up the Hudson, the shore was lined with people cheering and waving.

Jack volunteered to take on the job as tour director. He's is the smartest person I've ever met—it's like he's a walking Google. He memorized all of the statistics, including crew size, tonnage, height, armaments and other statistics for all ships in the strike group. He directed his assistant to prepare a handout for all visitors, explaining the details of the ships.

I had been aboard for only a half hour when I called Father Rick.

"Welcome aboard, Father! Were you saving this as a surprise?"

He roared with laughter.

"I love to keep old friends guessing," he said.

"Come on up to my office, Father. Jack and I are dying catch up with you."

When Father Rick walked into my office, military protocol disappeared. Although he held the Navy rank of captain, he exchanged bear hugs with me and Jack.

"We thought you had retired, Father," Jack said. "We even went to your retirement dinner. So what brings you back to sea?"

"Well, the Episcopal Archdiocese asked me to take over a new parish, but the transfer won't happen for over a year, so I found myself spending time helping my replacement in Norfolk learn the ropes. Then I got a call from my old friend, Charlie Singer, the assignment officer at the Bureau of Personnel. He asked me if I could come out of retirement for the upcoming deployment of the *Reagan* and Strike Group 2311. I missed my old Navy, so I jumped at the chance, especially when I heard that my good friend, Ashley Patterson, would be in command of the group. Hey, you two look great. I get a real kick when I see a couple who I married still happy and in love. When we met during the crazy *Gray Ship* incident, I just knew that you would be together forever."

"It's great to have you aboard, Father, and I know I speak for Jack too. When we went through that *Gray Ship* event, you and Jack were my advisors, and you're about to repeat that assignment. Having you two aboard helps calm my screaming stomach."

I was serious. You've heard the phrase, it's lonely at the top. It's true, especially when you command enough fire power to blow up a large city. But now two of my favorite people are with me.

This was my third Fleet Week, my first as an admiral. As we steamed down the Hudson, Matt Lauer, the host of NBC's *Today Show*, was aboard to interview me.

"Admiral Patterson," said Lauer, "you're the youngest admiral in the United States Navy, and you're also a woman, an

African-American woman. Can you tell us if you feel pressure beyond the normal stress of a military commander?"

"Matt, I consider myself a Navy line officer, nothing more, nothing less. I take orders and I give them. And most important of all, I follow my training, but sometimes you face decisions that you weren't specifically trained for. That's when I earn my paycheck. I don't think of myself as a woman (I lied); I think of myself as an admiral. The Navy has given me a job to do and I'm going to do it. Thank you for having me on your show, and thank you for headlining Fleet Week."

Matt Lauer left the ship by helicopter and flew to his next assignment.

CHAPTER FOUR

Fleet Week seemed like it was years ago, not days. Maybe that's because we just hit a wormhole and traveled through time.

I was having a hard time adjusting to our new reality of life in the distant past—or the distant future. Wouldn't you? Ever since we crossed the wormhole, my every waking moment was consumed with getting a grip on a new version of reality, as was everyone else on the *Reagan*. I began this deployment with the jitters of a new command. I now had the nerve-wracking job of figuring out where the hell we are and what year we're in. Okay, time to suck it up. It's time to address the crew.

After the bosun's pipe stopped, the quartermaster of the watch leaned into the microphone and said: "Attention all hands, attention all hands, attention to Admiral Ashley Patterson."

"Good morning my fellow crewmembers of the *USS Ronald Reagan*. First I will give you an update on Captain Tomlinson. As you may have heard, he suffered a heart attack and is recuperating in sick bay. Commander Molloy, our medical officer, assures me that the captain is doing well." (*Bullshit, I thought. Last time I saw Harry he looked horrible.*)

"If rumors were liquid," I continued, "this ship could float on rumors alone. (*That got a few laughs. So far so good.*) Since yesterday, we've been awash in rumors, or scuttlebutt as we call them in the Navy. I would normally address you as fellow crewmembers of Carrier Strike Group 2311, but as you all know, our strike group is down to one ship, the *Reagan*.

"At 0845 yesterday, daylight turned black and then turned light again in two minutes. The lovely scenery we saw on Long Island was gone, as were the other three ships of our strike group. That's what happened, plain and simple. You may have a hard time believing what I'm about to say, but it's the truth. We slipped through a slice in time itself, through a phenomenon known as a wormhole. Yes, that's right, we have traveled through time. As some of you may have read, I've experienced this phenomenon before. My deputy chief of staff, my husband Jack Thurber, has gone through it as well on a number of occasions. Father Rick Sampson has also time traveled. It's a difficult phenomenon to explain and understand, but I'll try. Think of a wormhole as a time portal, an actual place on earth like a slit or opening in time itself. We know we're not in the year 2017, the year we came from. But that's all we know. As of now, we have no idea what year we're traveling in. Judging from the disappearance of the homes on Long Island, we're theorizing that we're in the far distant past, or it could be the far distant future. Without asking anyone, I already know your question. How do we get back to where we came from? We all want to know the answer to that. So here's the answer, although it's not simple. My husband, Lieutenant Jack Thurber, wrote the definitive book on time travel a few years ago. He interviewed a lot of people who have experienced the phenomenon. There is a clear consensus on one point: To go back to where you came from, you simply cross over the wormhole again. It's that simple. But now it gets complicated. As you all felt, we were aground when we hit the wormhole. Our charts were way off from our actual depth reading. Because we were only touching bottom, our bow and stern thrusters were able to push us into deep water so we could maneuver. But the big concern is this: We were at high tide when the event happened. Crossing back through the wormhole without water under us will be a challenge to say the least. But I assure you that we are addressing this problem.

"So what is our mission? Obviously it's changed from our planned deployment to the Persian Gulf. Our job now, based on our new reality, is to find people and to link up with them so we can determine, first of all, what year we're in. Once we have made contact, we'll then address the most important mission—going home. Right now we're setting our course back to New York City. Lieutenant Thurber, our resident expert on time travel, will be giving you updates on the ship's TV station from time to time. Meanwhile, we can all try to learn a new skill—how not to check email every few minutes. (*That brought a few laughs, but not as many as I'd have liked*).

That is all. God bless you and God bless the *USS Ronald Reagan.*"

CHAPTER FIVE

W e turned the ship and set our course toward the entrance of New York Harbor. I went to sick bay to check on the condition of Captain Tomlinson. First I stopped by the medical office. In the Navy, don't expect a lot of privacy when you're sick. As the commander of the strike group, and acting commanding officer of the *Reagan*, I didn't need "next of kin" clearance to get the report on Tomlinson's condition.

"The captain's had a heart attack, admiral," said Molloy. "I won't classify it as a massive heart attack, but it was a serious cardiac episode. His job now is to get a lot of rest, a month at bare minimum, before he can resume his normal command. So you're our boss for the time being, ma'am. You can see him now. Just please don't talk about anything too exciting."

Don't talk about anything too exciting? We hit a friggin wormhole, went aground, found ourselves in God-only-knows-what-year, and this guy doesn't want me to talk about anything exciting?

"Harry, you look a lot better than the last time I saw you," I lied. "How are you feeling?"

"I feel like a dead weight, admiral, but better than yesterday. Doc Molloy tells me that I had a heart attack. I guess I'm not the first captain to have a cardiac episode when going aground, not to mention seeing darkness in daytime."

"Have you been brought up to date on what's happened to us?" I asked, poking around for some non-exciting things to talk about.

"Yes ma'am. It's been the only topic of conversation around here. Have we really traveled through time?"

"Yes, we have, Harry, and I'll fill you in on all the details as you get better. But for now I'm going to say something I never say to an officer under my command: Relax and rest, and don't worry about anything."

"Well, ma'am, having Admiral Ashley Patterson in command of my ship is a calming thought. If you need to see me about anything, ignore these medical people and come right on down."

"I'll do that Harry. Now get some rest."

⇥ ⇤

I ordered the navigator to steam at a moderate speed, no more than 20 knots. Since we had no idea where the hell we were in time, our job was to observe and record. I dialed the number for Lysle Phillips, commander of our air wing. He was also in charge of our drones. We carried five RQ-8 Fire Scout helicopter drones as well as six fixed-wing Predator drones. In the situation we find ourselves, unmanned aircraft are a blessing. While we steamed off the coast, our drones would surveil the land for signs of God-knows-what.

"Good morning, admiral."

"Good morning, Lysle, please have a seat. Coffee?"

"Yes, please, ma'am. Caffeine helps me to keep on my toes, which is where I have to be right now."

"Lysle, for the near future, drones will be our primary means of air ops. I say the near future, because I haven't the foggiest idea what the far future holds. After our little wormhole event, we saw that the buildings on Long Island were no longer there. We haven't seen any signs of life ashore; no smoke, no sound, nothing moving. Our drones are going to help us know what we're up against. I want at least one Predator and one Fire Scout helicopter paralleling our position at sea as they fly over the land. Put a couple of your best people in front of the video monitors. If anything looks interesting, alert me immediately. As you know, we have no idea what year we're in. We don't know if we're in some prehistoric time or far into the future. We just don't know, but it's our job to find out. Launch the drones immediately."

We steamed slowly toward New York City with Long Island off to starboard. Long Island, a highly populated region, was now a deserted forest. The weather was clear with a few high clouds. That's all I knew about the weather, what I can see outside the porthole in my office. We no longer got weather reports, and we couldn't call anybody to find out if a front was moving in. We couldn't call because we had nobody to call. We were on our own.

The drones patrolled over the land on a parallel course to ours. But all they were seeing were trees and an occasional field.

"Admiral, I want to increase altitude so we can get a broader look."

"Very well, commander."

Phillips had a good idea. The higher the drones flew the more we could see of the land below. From a height of one mile, we could see distinct geometric shapes, long lines of square shapes. We could also see three straight patterns running east to west. Could I be looking at the Long Island Expressway, the Northern State Parkway, and the Southern State Parkway? No roadway was visible, just overgrown vegetation, but the lines were there. The geometric shapes we saw could have been the foundations of buildings.

"Lysle, I think we're looking at the past, the distant past," I said.

"I concur, ma'am."

Suddenly there appeared on the screen a large herd of bison. My God, there must have been a thousand of them. I grew up in the borough of Queens in New York City, but it's geographically part of Long Island. The sight of bison roaming the fields of Long Island as if we were in Wyoming stunned me. It was just another thing that shouldn't be. Bison on Long Island! Once, while we spent a few days at our apartment in Manhattan, Jack and I decided to visit the farmland of Long Island's North Fork to do some pumpkin picking. I recalled seeing a small bison ranch in Riverhead. The owner of the ranch raised the animals for meat. He had a restaurant in town where bison burgers were a hit. Could these creatures have something to do with that ranch?

Our internal navigation system gave us constantly updated positions. But when I'd look at our position on a chart, it didn't conform to what I saw outside the bridge. There were no navigational aides, such as a church steeple or a flag pole. There were no buoys to mark channels. There was nothing.

Our charts told us one thing, but our eyes told us something else.

We would soon enter New York Harbor, or at least that's what it said on the chart. As any modern warship, the *Reagan* is equipped with the best sonar available. It was "forward looking" technology, meaning that we could see what's coming up, not just what's below us. As an extra precaution, I dispatched a couple of our helicopters to drop sonobuoys ahead of us. These are small buoys equipped with sonar, used primarily in anti-submarine warfare. They're also great for avoiding surprises. When you're driving a 101,000 ton ship with charts you can't rely on, you don't like surprises. Like most people, not just as a career Navy type, I love to be at sea and look at the sights ashore. But there were no sights to see, except for bison.

I called the OOD on the intercom. "Lieutenant, I'm going to catch a couple of winks. Call me if you see anything." I had slept very little in the past two days, and I desperately needed to close my eyes.

"Aye aye, admiral."

I stretched out on the couch and was asleep in less than a minute.

"Admiral Patterson, please come to the bridge," the OOD yelled, as if something just bit him on the ass.

I splashed cold water on my face, dried it off, and stepped onto the bridge, just a few feet away from my sea cabin.

"Look at that ma'am."

I felt like I was going to faint. The OOD was pointing to the wreckage of a bridge, old and rusty wreckage. From our chart location, it was, or rather it used to be, the Verrazano-Narrows Bridge, connecting Brooklyn to Staten Island. Oh, my God, I thought. This nails it. We've traveled into the future—far into the future. We had passed under the bridge not two days before. It had recently undergone a paint job and looked almost new. Now, all that remained was one of the towers, and the wreckage of rusted cables hanging alongside.

"Order all engines stop," I said to the OOD. The bridge was like a morgue. Not a sound. We all stared at something that couldn't possibly be, a ruin from long ago. But two days ago wasn't long ago.

I grabbed for a phone.

"Jack, please come to the bridge, honey."

I really have to stop talking that way, but at least I spoke softly. I don't think anybody heard me. I don't think. Screw it, I have bigger things to worry about than whether I call my honey, honey.

Jack walked up next to me. All I did was point.

"Dear God," Jack said, "Dear God almighty." Jack is a pretty religious guy. I knew he meant that as a prayer.

Jack looked around, as we all did. He noticed something that we hadn't, a small part of the Staten Island side of the bridge's towers poking just above the water. It was bent over and gnarled like a fist.

Jack looked at me and said, "That thing looks like it *melted*."

How do you melt a gigantic tower on a suspension bridge? I thought. The answer was obvious. It must have been a nuclear explosion, a nuclear explosion from long ago.

"Hey, I've got an idea," said Jack.

God bless him, he always has ideas.

"That guy who works in the engineering department, Lieutenant Bill Shaffer, who I had lunch with the other day during Fleet Week, used to be a metallurgist. Maybe he can tell us something more specific about what we're looking at. Jack picked up the phone and called Shaffer to the bridge.

I watched the blood drain out of Shaffer's face when I pointed out the bridge tower. "Can you help us understand what we're looking at lieutenant?"

"Just put me in a small boat so I can get a closer look, admiral. I don't have a lab here, but if I do some scraping I may be able to give you a rough estimate of how old that thing is, a very rough estimate based on layers of metal decay."

Shaffer climbed into an inflatable boat along with two Marines. I had just announced as ship's policy that nobody could leave the ship without an armed Marine escort. After Shaffer scraped metal shavings off the standing tower, they motored over to the one that was barely visible on the Staten Island side. Including the ride to and from, Shaffer was done with his scraping in an hour. He returned to the bridge.

"As I said Admiral, I can't give you an exact estimate without a metallurgy lab to back me up, but based on the levels of decay, I'm going to say that the wreckage we're looking at is at least 200 years old, maybe 250."

"So, based on what you just said, we could be in the 23rd Century."

Shaffer was sweating heavily. So was I. So was everybody on the bridge. And the temperature was about 63 with low humidity. I think our bodies were trying to reject our new reality.

"Any thoughts on the other structure, lieutenant, the one that looks like it melted."

"Yes, admiral, it definitely melted, and we all know what that means. This was the site of a nuclear blast, a nuclear blast from about 200 years ago."

"Thank you lieutenant. Please do a written report and give it to Lieutenant Thurber. He's cataloging all of our findings."

Jack looked at me. "I didn't know I was doing that, but it's an excellent idea."

"Who better than you, babe, I mean lieutenant."

I ordered the helicopters to drop sonobuoys between the towers. I didn't want the ship to scrape along any metal wreckage.

"All ahead one third, lieutenant," I said to the OOD. "We're going to continue our New York City investigation."

⇥ ⇤

In a few minutes we came upon what used to be the Battery, the southernmost tip of Manhattan Island. It looked like the cover of a dystopian novel. The Freedom Tower, the proud replacement for the Twin Towers that fell on 9/11, had been taken low by what we assumed was a nuclear explosion. It once stood at a towering 1,776 feet. Now it couldn't be more than 200 feet high. It was surrounded by small jumbles of wreckage.

When we looked south, we could see the tower on which the Statue of Liberty once stood. It was now just a tower, or rather half a tower. Part of it had crumbled to the ground. A huge hill of vegetation covered what was once, presumably, the Statue of Liberty herself.

"Admiral Patterson, this is Commander Philips in Air Ops. Please look at what one of our drones is picking up."

I looked at the video monitor and saw a pack of wolves scampering through the wreckage.

"I wonder what they eat," Jack said.

"I don't even want to think about that at the moment," I said.

"Admiral, look at the top of the screen at about two o'clock," Phillips said.

A small herd of sheep munched patches of vegetation.

"Looks like the wolves are about to have lunch," said the OOD.

"Thank you, commander," I said to the air boss. "Let me know if you pick up anything else."

We slowly proceeded north up the Hudson. I was surprised by the depth of the water, not as shallow as I'd expected. But I was starting to learn not to expect anything, just observe and record. Jack and I own (*own or once owned?*) a building in Manhattan, a lovely place on Fifth Avenue, bought by Mr. Moneybags Jack before we married. I grew up in Queens, just over the East River. It was sickening to see what had become of a city we loved.

"Commander," I said to the air boss, "increase altitude on the drones so we can get a wider view."

Manhattan was a wasteland, as simple as that. I saw what might have been the Empire State Building at one time, but was now just a small mountain of rubble. Around the mid-town area we could see the outline of a crater, obviously from a bomb that exploded near the ground. The skyscrapers that gave Manhattan it's once beautiful vistas were now part of a forest. I ordered the drone to fly up the East River.

As we passed what would have been 54th Street, Jack and I looked at each other. Our beautiful brownstone on Fifth Avenue and 54th Street was somewhere out there in the rubble and forest. During Fleet Week, Jack and I hosted a small cocktail party at our brownstone. I recalled walking along Fifth Avenue, heading toward our apartment. That was only five days ago.

We continued north toward the George Washington Bridge. From a distance of two miles we could see that the roadway had collapsed. Both towers were still erect, along with the graceful suspension cables. Apparently the open structure of the towers' frames enabled them to withstand the shockwaves of the bomb blasts. The vertical cables that once held the roadway were now rusted tendrils and swayed gently in the light breeze.

I ordered the drone to fly across Manhattan to Queens. I wanted to see the Bronx-Whitestone Bridge. There it was, both towers still standing, along with the suspension cables. The roadway had collapsed and the cables hung free, just like the George Washington Bridge. I turned toward Jack.

"I grew up a half mile from that bridge in Whitestone," I said softly, tears streaming down my face. Not very command-like, I thought. Fuck it. This was my home. Now it's rubble.

"Turn us around and head south commander," I said to the navigator. "We've seen enough. I want to patrol the eastern coastline to see if anything remains. Set a course for Baltimore."

In my position, it's important to keep up appearances, a display of military leadership. When you're in charge, it's important to show the troops that you have the situation in hand, to put on a poker face. I felt like crying, but I held it in to keep up command appearance. To see the city where you grew up turned into a forest inhabited by wolves is not a pleasant way to spend your morning.

CHAPTER SIX

Day Three

At 0800 I told Mike Blakely, my executive officer, to call a meeting of department heads in the wardroom at 0900. I figured it was important that the ship's leadership be up to the minute with our strange adventure.

Jack and I sat in my office before the meeting.

"Honey," I said to Jack, "you and I have been through some weird shit before, but this one really worries me. In every time travel event, the ones you and I went through, and the ones you went through without me, there's always one common theme, am I correct?"

"I assume you're talking about the way back, yes?"

"Yes, the way back. It always sounded so simple, didn't it Jack? Just find the wormhole and cross through it and you're back to where you came from. In our little adventure to World War II, which we nick-named *The Skies of Time*, we had a challenge to find the wormhole, because we flew through it in a plane. But we eventually found it. In the *Gray Ship* incident, we didn't have a reliable navigational fix for the portal, so we just steamed back and forth for two nauseating weeks until we hit it. But this one's a bitch. We were almost hard aground when we hit the goddam thing, and we struck it at high tide, what you could call the 'best case scenario.' I know you've been thinking about this, Jack. Everyone has. But how the hell can we steam through a wormhole when there's no water under us?"

"Ashley, until we come up with a revolutionary idea we have to recognize that the *Reagan* may never return to where she came from. We may have to cross the wormhole in groups in small boats. Chances are, we're going to have to leave the *Reagan* behind."

It will be interesting for me to explain to the Navy how I managed to lose an aircraft carrier.

"So you're going to be blunt with the department heads at the meeting?" Jack asked.

"Yeah, blunt. This weird situation screams out for transparency. I don't want people guessing what my next move will be. After the meeting I'm going to address the crew. I want you right by my side to feed me notes in case I leave anything out."

"I've already prepared your speech. Here it is."

I wasn't surprised. Jack has a way of thinking three steps ahead of anything I do.

⚔ ⚔

Mike Blakely, the XO, called the meeting to order at 0900.

"Folks," I said, "I don't want anybody guessing, and I don't want any speculating. We've just gone through two bizarre days. We've convinced ourselves that New York City was destroyed by nuclear attacks, as long as 200 years ago, maybe more. As I say those words, I can barely comprehend what I'm saying, but we have to go with the evidence that's in front of us. Yes, it appears that we've time traveled 200 years into the future. But what we don't know is this:

How did the future get to be this way? It's our obligation as military officers to find out as much as we can before we attempt to return to where we came from. I've spoken to a few of you individually, and I'm pretty sure we're all on the same page. As an admiral, I'm not simply going to bark out orders. Our lives have changed, and the only way we're going to get through this is by transparency and clear thinking. Here is the mission, and yes, it's open to discussion. We are going to steam for one month along the east coast of the United States, although we don't know if the land is still called the United States. We have one objective: to find human beings and communicate with them. If we can't find any living human beings, we'll have to assume that the world as we knew it came to an end about 200 years ago. Questions, comments?"

"Admiral," said the XO Mike Blakely, "can we discuss our plan for trying to find our way back? I think that's what everybody's thinking about."

"Of course, Mike," I said. "We touched on it at our last meeting. Since then we've all had time to think about our problem. So let me first nail down exactly what our problem is. As you heard from both me and my husband, Jack, the way to get to the other side of a wormhole is to go back and cross the same wormhole. But we all know that's a problem, possibly an insurmountable one as far as the *Reagan* is concerned. When we hit the wormhole we were almost hard aground. We actually *were* aground, just not dug in. Thank God our bow and stern thrusters were able to push us off into deep water. What makes the problem potentially insurmountable, and I'm open to suggestions, is that we were aground at high tide. In other words, it won't get any better. Now, because we have a fairly exact navigational fix, we should be able to find the wormhole without too much difficulty, but of course we can't do that because we won't have deep water to maneuver in. Long Island's South Shore is a historic graveyard of ships because littoral drift changes the sand's depth, and we may be looking at 200 years of changes in depth. The solution appears obvious, according to Jack. We're going to have to cross the wormhole in groups in small boats."

"We have enough small craft of various sizes to carry everybody," Jack said. "The Admiral's Barge, which I've always thought was a silly name, is really more like a pleasure yacht. It's about 40 feet in length and can hold two dozen people. There are five shore excursion boats. We have a dozen other small motor boats for use by the Marines, as well as a dozen inflatable boats and 50 survival craft. It will be a tight squeeze, but we can accommodate everybody."

"We also have a combination of 90 fixed wing aircraft and helicopters," Air Wing Commander Phillips said. Maybe a good part of the air group could *fly* through the wormhole."

I was amazed, that after just two days, my colleagues were thinking in terms of something that should be impossible—time travel. They talked about a wormhole as they would talk about a harbor entrance.

"Folks," I said, "after this meeting our return trip problem seems a lot less impossible. Okay, for the first part of our mission, we're going to look for people ashore. Now I have a special announcement to make. Father Rick Sampson, our chaplain, will be conducting a prayer service on the hangar deck in 15 minutes. It will be a memorial service for the repose of the souls of New York City."

I bit my lip as I said those words. A memorial service for a long dead city—the city where I grew up.

CHAPTER SEVEN

Day Four

Captain Harry Tomlinson was still recovering from his heart attack in sick bay. I visited him every morning. Despite the assurances from the medical officer, I thought Harry looked terrible.

Day four of our journey found us off the New Jersey coast, abeam of Atlantic City, the once popular gambling and entertainment mecca. The tall hotels and casinos were visible, if not quite gleaming.

"Slow down to 10 knots, lieutenant, order right full rudder," I said to the OOD. We had seen some buildings during our trip south, but Atlantic City actually *looked* like a city. Jack and XO Mike Blakely stood next to me on the open air wing of the bridge.

"I want to send a Marine platoon ashore to visit Atlantic City," I said. "Any thoughts?"

"It will be a crap shoot, admiral," Blakely said.

"Very funny, wiseass. Let's take a look at the drone video monitor."

The difference between what we saw of Atlantic City on the real time video and what we saw over New York City was dramatic. The only wreckage of buildings seemed to come from the passage of time and the normal decay of metal buildings along the sea shore. But one thing was the same. We saw no people, just the ever-present wolves, and plenty of sheep, bison, and other ungulates.

"Major Tucker to the bridge," the OOD said on my order. Major Clark Tucker was the commander of our Marine detachment.

"Major," I said. "I want you to send a platoon ashore to take a closer look at what we're seeing."

"That's Atlantic City, isn't it ma'am?"

"Yes, it is, and it appears to have escaped any direct nuclear blasts like the ones that hit New York. I don't have any suggestions for what you should look for, other than to keep your eyes and ears open. I want you to take Chief Petty Officer Dennis Ciano, the Master at Arms with you. He's a former detective with the NYPD and he knows what to look for. Also take Lieutenant Bill Shaffer, the metallurgist guy. Make sure that each Marine has an M16 with extra magazines. Those wolves look hungry."

I ordered the anchor dropped. A small platoon of 15 marines, led by Lieutenant Jake Patton, climbed into a shore tender. They were accompanied by Chief Dennis Ciano and Lieutenant Shaeffer, the metallurgist. For the purpose of the mission, they would be called *Platoon Bravo*. The boat was skippered by Petty Officer Second Class Dominic Morgante. He was a boatswain's mate and handled the craft with the skill he had learned working in his father's boatyard as a kid. He maneuvered the boat away from the platform off the port side of the *Reagan*. He looked at Lt. Patton. "It feels good to get away from the ship, don't you think, lieutenant?"

"Hey, it's only been four days. Are you a deep water sailor or what?"

"After what we saw in New York City, lieutenant, I feel like it's been a lifetime."

"I hear you, sailor. This is going to be an interesting trip."

They motored along the pier for a half hour, trying to find a suitable place to tie up. Most of the pier had rotted over the years and hung at various angles into the water.

"There's a stretch of open beach right there," said Patton. "Let's put the bow of the boat on the sand and tie her up."

"Okay, Marines, we're here for reconnaissance. If you see anything you consider interesting just make a note into your recording device. The time now is 1015. We'll rendezvous back here at 1500. Chief Ciano and Lt. Shaffer will be with me. Okay, move out."

"Ever been to Atlantic City before, lieutenant?" Ciano said, as they walked toward the buildings. They had to pick their way carefully through mounds of debris. The famous Atlantic City Boardwalk had long ago decayed into rubble.

"This will be my third time. But I don't expect to have as much fun as my last visit. Say, Chief, I understand that you used to be a detective with the NYPD. Where did you work out of?"

"Manhattan South," said Ciano.

"That view of Manhattan yesterday must have been quite a shock, I'm guessing."

Ciano glanced at Patton.

"I don't want to talk about it, lieutenant. I don't want to fucking talk about it."

Chief Dennis Ciano was a big man. At 6'4," he had the build of a defensive tackle, with sandy blond hair, and a gruff manner of speaking. He also had a keen eye for evidence.

Patton turned on his recorder and began making observations.

"This is Lt. Jake Patton of the United States Marine Corps. I'm here in Atlantic City, New Jersey, on orders from Admiral Ashley

Patterson of the *USS Ronald Reagan*. I'm leading a platoon of 15 Marines. Our job is reconnaissance: to look, listen, and report. We're also accompanied by Chief Petty Officer Dennis Ciano, the Master at Arms for the *Reagan*. Chief Ciano is a former detective with the NYPD. I'm also with Lt. Shaffer of our engineering department. Lt. Shaffer was once a metallurgist. I'm looking at a scene of devastation, but nothing like what we saw yesterday in New York City. We've been told by senior command that we may be 200 years into the future. The damage to the buildings here appears to be from the ravages of time, not a nuclear blast. I'm asking Lt. Shaffer to weigh in."

"Yes," Shaffer said, "we're seeing the effects of age, maybe 200 years. Buildings that aren't maintained will eventually rot, and that's what happened to these structures. I see no evidence of heat blast, such as from a nuclear weapon. I remember that TV special on the History Channel a few years ago called *Life After People*. It was a documentary that speculated about what happens to cities if there are no people around to maintain them. That's what this place reminds me of. "

"Chief, any comments?"

"One thing that catches my eye is the remnants of car accidents," Ciano said. "In my range of vision I count no fewer than seven collision sites, and three of them involve more than two vehicles. They're rusted hulks, of course, but they are definitely vehicles. It looks like a lot of people were trying to get out of town—*fast*."

"Let's go into that casino," said Patton. "I think I can see some retail stores. Maybe we can find a newspaper or magazine."

"*Freeze*" screamed Ciano as he opened fire with his fully automatic M16. Four wolves lay dead 20 feet from them.

"Those fuckers were coming right at us," Ciano said. "They had no fear at all."

Patton reached for his radio.

"*Platoon Bravo* this is Lt. Patton. We've just been attacked by four wolves. They came straight at us with no apparent fear. Thanks to

Chief Ciano, we're okay. Keep your weapons at the ready and keep your eyes open."

They walked into the casino. The floor was littered with broken glass and debris from years of howling wind off the ocean. Wolf droppings covered a large part of the floor. Apparently the wolves seek shelter in the casino when it's cold outside. About 20 shops lined the lobby, most with broken glass windows.

"I suggest we take a look at the casino itself," said Ciano. "It's right over there."

They walked into a sea of slot machines and gaming tables.

"You guys tell me what you see," Ciano said.

"Well, at the risk of appearing obvious, Chief, I see a bunch of slot machines and card tables."

"What else?" Ciano asked.

"Chips," said Patton. "Chips as far as the eye can see. A lot on the floor, mostly covered with moss, and a lot piled on the card tables."

"Do you guys gamble?" Chief Ciano asked.

They both shook their heads.

"I seldom do myself, but I've been on a lot of investigations involving gambling, and this room screams at me. A real gambler, such as my asshole cousin, would never dream of leaving chips laying around without cashing them in. It would be like a fish forgetting how to swim. A real gambler would fucking die before he'd leave his chips behind. Something happened to scare the hell out of these people. My guess is that they heard about the nukes in NYC. These people got out of Dodge fast, too fast for a gambler unless he was scared shitless."

Ciano dictated his observations into his recorder.

"This is Chief Ciano," he dictated into his recorder. "We're now entering a large facility that appears to have been a stationery and book store at one time. Remnants of books and magazines are neatly lined up along the shelves, although in varying degrees of decomposition. None of the covers are legible. I opened a couple of the books, and the typeset is slightly visible. None of the magazines or newspapers are even vaguely readable."

"Hey, look at this," said Lt. Shaffer. "It looks like a plastic bin for newspaper storage."

He opened the bin. "Holy shit," yelled Ciano. "These newspapers look okay."

"My guess is that they kept the next day's newspapers in this bin before putting them on the shelves," said Shaffer.

"Freeze!" shouted Patton. He raised his M16 and fired a short burst at a wolf that had just loped into the store.

Ciano shook his head and picked up the top newspaper, *The New York Times.*

"Are you guys ready for the date? April 12, 2018, less than a year after we shoved off on our deployment. And check out the headline. It looks like the largest typeface the *Times* ever uses."

Nuclear Talks between Iran and the United States Falter
Reports of large amounts of Iranian weapons delivered to North Korea
President puts Military on High Alert

"My God," said Patton. "I guess we're looking at the reason these newspapers were never put on the shelves the next day. April 12, 2018—the day the world ended."

Platoon Bravo rendezvoused on the sand next to the boat. As they waited for the rest of the platoon, the sounds of machine gun bursts broke the still air.

"These wolves never got the fucking memo," said Sergeant Martinez, "the memo that said, 'avoid men with guns.' "

That afternoon *Platoon Bravo* boarded the *Reagan*. I ordered them to report to my office, where Jack, XO Blakely, and I awaited.

"We think we know what happened many years ago, admiral," said Patton. He placed the *New York Times* in front of me. I read the front page, with Jack and Mike Blakely over my shoulder.

"Oh dear Lord," I said, "April 12, 2018, the day that ended history. I guess this headline explains what the nuclear bombs were all about, especially New York City. Give me your impressions of Atlantic City, fellas," I said.

Patton gestured to Ciano. "Admiral, I'll defer to our resident detective, Chief Ciano."

"The place was evacuated, admiral, and was evacuated fast," Ciano said. "I guess that headline explains why. We saw few skeletal remnants, not exactly surprising if our 200-year estimate is correct. From the numerous car accidents and the fact that thousands of dollars in gambling chips were left lying around, I think we just looked at a city that emptied in an instant. We're guessing that the people from Atlantic City heard about what happened to New York, and decided to run."

"Good work, fellas," I said. "I'm not sure I'm happy with what you've found, but at least we have one answer."

I walked to the bridge.

"Weigh anchor, lieutenant," I said to the OOD. "Resume previous course and speed."

The traditional Navy theme song, "Anchors Aweigh," played over the ship's sound system, as was the custom any time we picked up the hook. I'd always loved that song, and it usually gave me a feeling of stirring pride. But I was beginning to feel numb with all of the shit we discovered. Maybe we should play "Helter Skelter."

Shortly, we passed Cape May, New Jersey, the southernmost tip of the Garden State. Jack and I once spent a weekend in Cape May, and we both fell in love with the place. It's a town of beautiful old Victorian homes, painted in their authentic colors. I should say it *was* a town like that. Because most of the structures were made of wood, the years of neglect returned most of them to the earth. From the drone videos we didn't see any evidence of blast damage, just crumbling old houses. No signs of human life. Wolf packs roamed the deserted streets, of course. I was feeling nostalgic for the past.

CHAPTER EIGHT

Nigel Portland stood on the front porch of his house overlooking what was once Arlington National Cemetery. His house was on land formerly owned by Robert E. Lee, hundreds of years in the past. Portland loved the association with a famous general, because he held that same rank, in the Eastern Empire, a rank he had conferred upon himself.

Portland was tall, at 6'1" and thin. He was 42 years old, but had steel gray hair, which he wore long. He could easily have been a hippy from the 1960s. He had piercing blue eyes, which many people found intimidating. Over his shoulder was strapped an M16, an old weapon, but still quite reliable.

The Eastern Empire, as the town was called for over a century, was once located in Gettysburg, Pennsylvania. The original settlers, 20 years after the *Big War*, choose Gettysburg because of its countless brass monuments to Confederate and Union soldiers. Besides the monuments, hundreds of old cannons lined what was once a battlefield. The monuments and cannons proved useful for melting down and refurbishing into parts for machinery.

A few of the original settlers objected to the destruction of the monuments and argued that they should be preserved for history. The leadership, under command of a man named James Wentworth, could see no reason why anyone would want to preserve history. Now is now, he thought. What use is history? The monuments were melted and the battlefields plowed under for crops.

In 2068, 50 years after the war, the inhabitants of the Eastern Empire moved the settlement to its present location in what was once Arlington, Virginia, next to Washington D.C. Washington had been destroyed in the war, and provided an endless supply of marble and granite from the rubble of the old government structures, valuable building material.

"Good morning, General Portland," said his aide, Lieutenant Joshua Billings, as he bounded up the steps. He gave the general a sharp salute, which Portland returned.

"Good morning, lieutenant," Portland said, "I know you like to chat, but I have some questions, especially about our readiness. Please bring me up to date."

"Yes, sir. Our strength level has improved in the past months. We now have just under 10,000 soldiers in the Army of the Eastern Empire. Our armaments are improving as well. As you know sir, we discovered that ancient arsenal which was once part of the United States Army. It was known as the Picatinny Arsenal from Morristown, New Jersey."

"Lieutenant I'm well aware of the name of the arsenal. I would rather that you tell me about our armaments."

"Yes, sir. All of the weapons are in excellent condition. They had been kept over the years in a lead-walled enclosure below ground level. We now have enough M16 automatic machine guns and pistols of various calibers to equip our entire army. We've also recovered thousands of rocket-propelled grenades and hundreds of grenade launchers."

"When does my staff recommend the next raid, and where will it be?"

"The staff recommends an attack on a settlement near what used to be Richmond, Virginia, now called Fortuna Town. The settlement is occupied by approximately 1,000 people. They are quite adept at farming, so we will acquire not only food, but the leaders we capture can help us with our supply needs in the future. Of course, many of the captives will wind up serving in the Army of the Eastern Empire."

"Are they protected, lieutenant? Do they have any armed forces guarding them?"

"Their armed force is quite minimal, general. We don't expect much of a fight and we don't anticipate many casualties."

"And when does the staff recommend the attack?"

"In two weeks, sir."

"Keep me apprised of any developments, lieutenant. Oh, and the next time you come before me, make absolutely certain that your uniform is ironed."

"Yes, sir."

Portland considered himself a military man, although he had never served in any armed force. But he did know how to control people, and how to secure their allegiance. He gave himself the title of general. He felt it was appropriate to a man of his stature. In another time, Nigel Portland would have been known simply as a warlord.

⋙⋘

"One other thing, general, if I may. One of our reconnaissance drones photographed a gigantic ship off Baltimore. Here is the photo."

"Do we have any idea what this ship is, lieutenant?"

"Yes, sir. I looked through an old encyclopedia we keep in one of our store rooms. It appears to be an aircraft carrier. You can see planes on the deck in the photo. We have no idea where this ship came from, or who it belongs to. If we had to confront this vessel it could be dangerous."

"Keep tracking the ship with at least one drone, Lieutenant. Report to me any changes in her course."

CHAPTER NINE

April 12, 2018

Grace Moynihan sat at the Bethesda Fountain Café in Central Park at 8:15 a.m. Her husband of 20 years had died of cancer two years ago. She awaited a man whom she just met three weeks before at a charity fundraiser, Phil McLaughlin. At age 45, Grace felt like a kid again, having been totally smitten with Phil, an IT manager with Sunoco. This was their third date. Phil was a widower of three years, having lost his wife to a car accident. Grace was also an IT manager, and was happy that she and her new friend had common professional lives, and a way to keep a conversation going in the early stages of a relationship. The temperature was 71 degrees, perfect for mid-April, and Grace had selected an outside table overlooking the fountain. Phil approached the table, smiling. She had no idea how to behave with someone she was attracted to, having been away from the dating scene for so long. She decided to follow her instincts. She stood, wrapped her arms around his neck, and hugged him. Phil's face turned red, one of the things that she found attractive about the man. He seemed like a guy with few pretenses, she thought. They sat, held hands, and looked into each other's eyes.

"Grace, I hope I'm not being too forward, but I have to confess that the past three weeks have been a shift in my life. Since I lost Jane, I've felt adrift, like I couldn't see beyond the next day. When I look at you, I see a future. Damn, I'm being entirely too forward, aren't I?"

"No, you're not," said Grace. "We're old enough to know what life is all about, and we're young enough to see that there can be a future for us."

Phil pulled his chair next to Grace. They stared into each other's eyes, and their faces moved slowly toward each other.

In the final moment of their lives, their lips touched.

The flash of the blast was all enveloping, turning the atmosphere into total whiteness. The explosion was followed within moments by the shock wave, an irresistible force of wind and debris that swept everything in its path, including skyscrapers. The bomb had detonated over 42nd Street, some thirty blocks away. At the same time, another bomb exploded over lower Manhattan, destroying the new Freedom Tower, the replacement for the Twin Towers that had succumbed to terrorism on 9/11. The Statue of Liberty was toppled as well, along with the canyons of lower Manhattan. Another bomb exploded over Queens, and a fourth over Brooklyn.

New York City was destroyed.

⊨+⊨

Lin Chu Lee, age 18, sat with his father and enjoyed an early morning tea at 5:15 a.m. on the deck of their Los Angeles home. The Lee family had a tradition of early rising. Normally a reticent man, Lin's father put down his tea and looked into his son's eyes.

"Lin Chu," his father said in his native Mandarin, "your mother and I couldn't be more proud of you. You will graduate from UCLA in a couple of months, and if you keep up your hard work, you will be first in your class. You have brought honor and pride to our family, and have a wonderful future before you."

Sunrise would not be until 6:15 a.m., so they enjoyed their tea in the gentle early morning light.

As Lin Chu raised his cup to his lips, the pre-dawn gloom became the brightest light he had ever seen. It would also be the last light he ever saw.

The shock wave of the explosion, coming moments after the flash, swept across Los Angeles, taking all structures with it. The lush Hollywood Hills, with hundreds of mansions of the rich and famous, soon became smoking mountains of radioactive debris.

Maria Protenza, age 22, walked into the cafeteria at the University of Chicago Law School at 7:15 a.m. During her three years in law school, Maria formed some habits, mostly good ones. An early riser, she relished the early morning hours before classes to review her casebook study from the night before. She ranked number five in her class, and she wanted to push it even higher before graduation in two months. Maria and her parents had come to the United States from Milan, Italy, when she was five years old. She was the eldest of six children. The Protenzas were a close family. Her parents spoke passable English, although the charming lilt of their native Italy lingered. The Protenzas owned a successful pizza restaurant near their home in the Bridgeport section of Chicago. The entire family was involved in working at Protenza Pizza, even the very youngest.

Maria was the first member of the Protenza family to graduate from college, a fact that Alonzo, her beaming father, would often tell customers. After she graduated from Northwestern University first in her class, her dad held a party that the people of Bridgeport still remembered. Maria tried not to take herself too seriously—that was the job of her fawning parents. Every day she wore a little button to class that read: "Eat Pizza-Live Longer."

She had just been offered a coveted job with the prestigious Chicago law firm, Winston and Strawn. She had to agree with her loving parents. Her future looked great.

The cafeteria was dimly lit. She sat under an overhead light to give her enough brightness for reading. The sudden flash that enveloped the cafeteria blinded her. She didn't see the wall of the cafeteria rushing toward her as the shock wave hit.

Three bombs were detonated over Chicago, one on the south side, the one that destroyed the university, one near the Willis Tower, once known as the Sears Tower, and one amidst the skyscrapers of Upper Michigan Avenue. The Willis Tower fell, along with most of the Michigan Avenue buildings.

⇒⊹ ⊹⇐

At 8:17 a.m. Eastern Time, President Reynolds sat at his desk in the Oval Office, meeting with Randy Jackson, his Chief of Staff. The door swung open and six Secret Service officers stormed in, one shouting, "We gotta go, Mr. President."

They surrounded both the President and Randy Jackson and hustled them into a private elevator which led to the White House basement. Neither the White House, nor its basement, was designed to survive a direct nuclear attack, but they slammed the hardened doors shut, providing a modicum of protection.

"What the fuck is going on?" President Reynolds shouted, well-known for his salty language.

"The nation is under a nuclear attack, sir," said the leader of the team. "New York, Chicago, and L.A. have received direct hits. We have to assume that Washington is on the list of targets."

"Where's Amanda?" Reynolds asked, referring to his wife, the First Lady.

Amanda Reynolds was led into the basement room by another group of Secret Service agents. The President and First Lady hugged, then looked into each other's eyes. Over the years, the Reynolds had a close and loving relationship. They continued to hold each other, expecting to die at any moment.

The first bomb detonated over the White House at 8:21 a.m.

CHAPTER TEN

Day Five

We steamed toward Baltimore. I chose that city because it's a major harbor and a center of commerce, or at least it was in 2017. Jack and my department head advisors have come up with the theory that New York City may have been the major target for the nuclear attacks, possibly the only one. I tentatively agreed, but I thought that Washington D.C. would have been an obvious target as well. Baltimore, not far from D.C., would give us the answer. The average depth of Chesapeake Bay is only 21 feet, but there is a deep water channel that runs most of the distance of the bay. The *Reagan* draws 37 feet, so we had to navigate carefully. We proceeded slowly, with helicopters dropping sonobuoys in front of us to keep an accurate fix on our depth. We were all working on the assumption that some people must have survived, an optimistic guess, but we had nothing to base it on. It was just a task of finding them, assuming anyone's there at all.

As we steamed up Chesapeake Bay toward the mouth of Baltimore Harbor, the OOD let out a shout.

"Holy shit, er sorry, admiral. There's a small water craft two points off the starboard bow."

When a person indicates the number of points off the bow he's using the relative bearing system, that is, relative to the vessel itself, not to the compass. It's a good method of pointing out something in the water. Each "point" is 11.25 degrees, so with practice, it's easy to spot an object in the water relative to the ship.

There it was. Through my binoculars it looked like a 25-foot Grady White, a popular fishing and pleasure boat (at least it was in 2017). The boat was about 200 yards away and heading straight for us. In hostile waters—and our operating assumption on this cruise was that *all* waters were hostile—a helicopter launched without my even having to order it. The *USS Cole* incident in 2000 changed a lot of naval security procedures.

"Turn right and then cut your engine or you will be fired upon," came the stern warning from the helo pilot over his loudspeaker. As the helicopter hovered, one of our inflatables pulled alongside the boat with two of Marines aboard.

"Prepare to be boarded," yelled one of the Marines.

Not "permission to come aboard," just "prepare to be boarded." The *Reagan* was on a war footing, so it was no time for maritime niceties.

The boat was inhabited by two rather fat people, a man and a woman. For some weird reason, they seemed almost happy that the Marines were boarding their vessel. Through my binoculars I could see that they were laughing.

"We're taking you aboard for questioning. Your boat will be hauled and kept safe," the Marine corporal said.

They maneuvered the inflatable with the Grady White in tow next to the loading platform on the *Reagan*. Their boat was hauled aboard by a crane and stowed on deck.

The Marines brought the two boaters to my office, as ordered. Jack was with me, along with XO Mike Blakely and Father Rick. My God, these two laugh a lot, we all agreed.

"Patana bana," the man said loudly, after which he cracked up laughing.

"I take it that you don't speak English," I said.

"Bitty, bitty," he said pinching his thumb and index finger together. I assumed he meant "a little bit." After he said that he cracked up, of course.

"What is your name?" I said.

"Me Pango, she Erl Girl."

"Well, it's a pleasure to meet you folks," I said, having no idea where this conversation was going.

"I'm Admiral Ashley Patterson and I'm in command of this ship. Are you from Baltimore?

"Yes, yes, Balti Balti."

He seemed to understand me, which is more than I could say of him.

"Let's speak slowly," I said, "so we can communicate better."

He laughed, no surprise. Then he shouted in a pleasant voice.

"Yo, Erl Girl. Saquanna puncha!"

With that she walked behind him and tugged on a zipper. Suddenly he was no longer a fat man. He wore blue jeans (blue jeans!) and a tee shirt. Actually he was quite slim and good looking.

Erl Girl stood in front of him and said, "Yo, Pango, Saquanna puncha," laughing as she said it.

Pango then walked behind Erl Girl and tugged down the zipper on the back of her clothes. Same result. She went from being an unattractive fat girl to a stunningly pretty, slender woman. She wore khaki slacks and a tight fitting tee shirt. Her hair was blond in a pixie cut.

I looked at Jack, Mike, and Father Rick.

"Can anybody tell me what just happened?"

They shrugged.

"Allow me to introduce ourselves properly, admiral. I'm Edward Monkton and this is my wife Margaret," our suddenly slim boater friend said.

"Jack, please pass me a glass of water," I said.

"Edward, can you please tell us what just happened?" I said "You two went from primitives who spoke in a strange patois to a couple of attractive people who speak perfect English."

"We're on scout duty, ma'am. Our job is to observe strangers and to report back to our superiors. Those ridiculous costumes we wore actually contain a mild narcotic that makes us laugh and speak strangely. The purpose is to mask our identity if stopped. It didn't take me long to determine that you people are not our enemy."

"Well, we're definitely not your enemy, but how did you know that?" I said.

"I am well aware of history, including the *USS Ronald Reagan*. We spotted you from shore and I did some fast research."

"Edward," I said, "before we go any further, I have a pressing question to ask you. What year is this?"

"You are in the year 2227, admiral. I don't know if that shocks you or not, because I know that you're time travelers."

"Yes, we are time travelers, and how you know that totally baffles me. That means that we came here from 210 years in the past. We had calculated 200, so we were close. We found an old newspaper from 2018 that convinced us that a nuclear war occurred in that year."

"Yes, it did, admiral. It was the end of a long civilization. Have you seen New York City?"

"Yes, we have. I grew up there. The sight of the devastation sickened me. But let me ask you, were any other cities attacked?"

"Yes, besides New York there were nuclear attacks on Los Angeles, San Francisco, Dallas, Atlanta, Chicago, and Washington D.C. The long-term devastation swept the country, the country once known as the United States."

"What's it named now?"

"Well there is no more *it*, if the *it* you refer to is the country you came from. Some call the region around here simply the

Eastern Empire, but nobody really knows. Baltimore is still called Baltimore, or Balti Balti if I'm wearing my crazy suit."

"I'm amazed at your detailed knowledge of the history of over 200 years ago," said Jack. "Where or how did you learn about all this?"

"To answer your question," said Margaret, "Edward and I should introduce you people to someone, a very important man."

CHAPTER ELEVEN

Jeremy Lang, the mayor of Miami Town, sat on the edge of his bed as he strapped on the prosthesis that replaced his left leg. Five years before, while swimming in the Atlantic, he was stung by a jellyfish. Like many small areas, Miami Town lacked all but the most rudimentary medical services. The medical personnel, to the extent they had any training, tried various remedies for the sting. Eventually the wound became gangrenous and his leg had to be amputated. The town had been founded 20 years earlier, in the year 2207 by Roberto Lang, Jeremy Lang's grandfather. The citizens of the town formed it after they experienced countless raids on their previous location 100 miles to the north. The population of Miami Town was 1539, not large enough to support a variety of occupations or skills.

The weather was oppressively hot and humid, which didn't help the mayor's discomfort with his prosthesis. There were legends about a technology called air conditioning, but no one had any idea how it might work.

Lang walked slowly down the sloping grass in front of his house. His office was in "town hall," a small building next to a lake. With the windows open, it provided a slight breeze, along with swarms of mosquitoes. He had assembled his "town council" for a meeting to discuss the town's business. Jeremy Lang called himself mayor, a title he believed was fitting for his position. As in most towns, he didn't rise to his office by an election. He killed his predecessor after a card game, and nobody else wanted the job.

Four men and three women sat around a conference table awaiting him. They formed his town council, each of whom he had appointed, including his mistress, Maria.

Jacob Lopez, one of the councilmen raised his hand. The meetings never began with a reading of the minutes of the prior meeting, because nobody kept minutes. The council members, the ones who knew how to read and write, would scribble notes to themselves as meetings progressed.

"Mr. Mayor," said Lopez, "I have been hearing constant suggestions that we may want to establish a police or security force of some sort. Robberies are on the increase and assaults happen every day. Just last week someone was murdered."

"Councilman Lopez," said Lang, with a sneer on his face. "We love to hear interesting ideas, but unless you can figure out a way to pay for the ideas, please don't raise them."

Miami Town didn't have a system of money, where currency could be exchanged for goods and services. The town operated on a system of barter, of either services or agricultural products from the small farms in the town. The town citizens, as well as the town council, were semi-literate at best. Mayor Lang couldn't read a word. Nobody was familiar with the idea of money, because nobody ever read history. A few books were discovered years ago in an old abandoned building. Owing to the humidity, the words in the books were barely legible, which didn't matter because there were so few people to read them. The books were used as kindle for fires on the occasionally chilly evening.

Miami Town had been largely destroyed in the *Big War.* The population that wasn't wiped out in the atomic blasts, died over the next few years of radiation poisoning and cancer. The current occupants of the area named the place Miami Town, because somebody found a road sign that read, "Welcome to Miami."

A constant threat to the town came from raiding parties from other small towns in the area. Councilman Lopez raised his hand again He felt a bit reticent, because he had just been rebuffed by Mayor Lang for suggesting a police force that couldn't be paid.

"Perhaps a police force could be voluntary, such as our army that fights off raiders."

Lang laughed. "And who would protect us from the police, assuming we could convince enough people to serve?" He gave Lopez a look that said he had heard enough.

Councilwoman Estrella Durang raised her hand.

"Mr. Mayor, it seems to me that our town is shrinking. Nobody keeps count, but perhaps we should start. I once heard of a position called 'town clerk,' a person in charge of that sort of thing. I'd be happy to volunteer, although I'm not sure what the job would be."

"That's an excellent idea Councilwoman Durang," said Lang. "I hereby appoint you Miami Town Clerk. Begin counting people and doing whatever else you think should be done. You will be paid with an extra weekly ration from the main town farm."

Councilwoman Durang had raised an important point, the dwindling population of Miami Town. Because of the low fertility rate of its citizens as well as the inadequate medical care, the population of Miami Town had actually shrunk by 50 percent in the past 10 years, although nobody noticed, except perhaps for Councilwoman Durang.

Miami Town was slowly dying.

CHAPTER TWELVE

Day Six

"Who is this person you want us to meet, Edward, and where is he? Baltimore?" I asked.

"We call him *The Samah*, which roughly translates to 'leader.' No he isn't in Baltimore, but around 250 miles west of our current position, a place that was once known as White Sulphur Springs, West Virginia. It's where Margaret and I live when we're not on scout duty here in Baltimore."

"White Sulphur Springs?" said Jack. "That's where the Greenbrier Resort is, or was, located. I remember that the government signed a contract with the resort to build a huge underground bunker as an emergency relocation facility for the government in case of a nuclear attack. I think they called it Project Greek Island. It was decommissioned in 1995, if I recall."

Who needs the Internet and Google when you have Jack around? I thought. I just squeezed his hand and smiled at him.

"It's still called the Greenbrier," Edward said, "and the bunker is still there. You'll find out more shortly."

"How did you get here?" I asked. "Two hundred and fifty miles is quite a distance."

"We used an old battery operated Jeep," Edward said.

"Is there a place to land a helicopter?" I asked.

"Yes, ma'am" said Edward. "There's a large lawn in front of the resort, which hasn't changed that much over the years."

"Great. Leave your Jeep here." I said. "You can pick it up at a later date. We'll take one of our *Sea King* helicopters. It has a range of over 600 miles, so we can get there and back without refueling. It should take us no more than an hour and a half. I'll pilot the helo to save a seat. Normally the thing can carry a pilot and three passengers, so we'll have an extra passenger. I want Jack and Father Rick to join us. We have a *Harrier* Jump Jet aboard that will provide combat air support. Because it takes off and lands vertically it won't need to use an airstrip and can park on the lawn next to the helo. Let's leave as soon as possible."

Jack walked over to a phone and dialed the air department, giving instructions to prepare a *Sea King* and *Harrier* jet for immediate take off. As usual, Jack was ahead of us.

"I imagine that you folks must find this ship amazing," I said as we awaited word that our aircraft were ready to launch.

"Yes, it is amazing technology, admiral," said Margaret. "This is the first time Edward and I have actually seen a real Nimitz Class carrier, except for books and videos. I understand the *Reagan* displaces 101,000 tons, and has a cruising range of over 25 years with its nuclear reactor."

I looked at Jack. This will be an interesting trip, I thought.

As we flew over land, I stared out the windshield. It was the first time I had a view of the ground other than from the drone video screens. Our helmets were equipped with radios so we could communicate over the sound of the rotors.

"Edward and Margaret." I said, "I can't help but notice that we haven't seen any signs of human life; no smoke, no vehicles, just forest."

"I can assure you, admiral," Edward said, "that there are people under the forest canopy. There are definitely people there, although not as many as you may expect. *The Samah* will fill you in on a lot more detail than Margaret and I have.

We could see the beautiful main building of the resort appear in front of us. The place had obviously been maintained over the years. It looked almost new from my vantage point. Although I had never visited the place before, I recalled it from photos. I set the *Sea King* down on the large lawn in front of the building, and the *Harrier* landed right next to us. Uh oh, I thought. I counted roughly 25 heavily armed men in uniforms of some sort. I looked at Edward.

"Please don't be concerned, admiral," said Edward. "We take security quite seriously here. They're expecting us."

We planned to stay for at least one night, so we all had bags with us. A group of six young men walked up to us to take our bags. Once a resort always a resort, I thought, except the bellmen usually don't pack machine guns.

Edward and Margaret escorted us through the main door of the building. I forced myself to have a blank mind about this *Samah* guy. Just let the facts flow and don't prejudge anything.

The inside of the building was as elegant as the exterior. Beautiful cherry wood panels adorned all of the walls. A large Persian rug took up most of the polished wooden floor. The furniture in the place is what you would expect in such opulent surroundings. Heavy leather chairs and couches were nestled in seating areas. A young woman approached us with a tray of coffee and tea. Edward asked us to be seated while he made a couple of calls to arrange for our stay.

"Let me show you folks to your guest rooms," said Margaret.

The guest rooms were as tastefully decorated as the main lobby. The room where Jack and I would stay had two private baths, and a beautiful view of the grounds through a large picture window. It suddenly felt good to be off the ship.

After we stowed our bags, Margaret took us back to the main lobby, where Edward awaited us. It was hard to think that just yesterday Edward and Margaret were a couple of weird looking primitives who spoke a strange language.

"We'll be leaving you folks here. *The Samah* will be with you momentarily," said Edward.

"*The Samah*," Father Rick said. "What's your guess, the guy will wear antlers and a long robe?"

He cracked up at his own joke, as did Jack and I.

"Maybe he'll wear a rubber fat suit and will say things like 'Saquanna puncha,' " Jack said.

I think we were cracking jokes and laughing because we were nervous about just who this *Samah* guy would be. I know *I* was nervous.

⋙ ⋘

A tall handsome man with gray-streaked black hair walked in with a tray of finger sandwiches. This was good, because the three of us were hungry. It was past lunch time. He put the tray on the mahogany table in front of us.

"Welcome to the Greenbrier" the man said. "Yes, we kept the old name. Kind of classy, no?" He let out a hearty laugh. The guy, who I figured was about 42 or 43, wore impeccable stylish clothes. Must be a high-end men's store around here, I guessed.

"So you must be Admiral Patterson. Edward and Margaret told me all about you."

"Yes, I am," I said. "This is my husband, Lieutenant Jack Thurber, and this is Father Rick Sampson, the ship's chaplain."

He grabbed each of our hands in a firm warm handshake.

Who the hell is this guy? I wondered. I figured I'd take a guess.

"Are you *The Samah*?" I asked.

He let out another laugh.

"Samah, Shmama! You folks can call me Bill. Some of my colleagues around here like to keep an air of mystery about me. I'm Bill Wellfleet, the proprietor of this establishment. I hope you like it."

Another hearty laugh. Getting to know this guy would be a work in progress, I decided.

"I don't know if Edward and Margaret had the time to tell you about us and our reason for being here," I said.

"Yes, they did. It took them about five minutes while you folks were putting your bags in your rooms. Only five minutes. You'll find that we think fast around here." Another laugh.

"So let me see if I have this straight," said Bill as he bit into a ham sandwich. "You people are all crewmembers of the *USS Ronald Reagan*. You have time traveled here from the year 2017 after you hit a wormhole off the coast of Long Island. How'm I doin' so far?"

"You've pretty much summarized it, Bill, but *we're* still confused. Are you familiar with time travel?"

"Yes, indeed," said Bill. "Time travel was once considered a dusty corner of science fiction, but over the years people have begun to understand that it is a very real phenomenon. Nobody has done more to educate people about time travel than your husband Jack here. I've read your book Jack—oh, is it okay if I call you Jack?"

"Of course," Jack said.

"Please give me your observations," Bill said, "and then I'll tell you all about *us.*"

"We knew what happened to us within moments of hitting the wormhole," I said. "Jack and I have experienced time travel before, and so has Father Rick. The buildings ashore simply disappeared, as did the other three ships from our group, known as Carrier Strike Group 2311. We knew we were in another time, but we didn't know if it was the distant past or the future. When we steamed to New York City and discovered the hulk of a destroyed bridge, we knew we were in the future. One of our engineers, who used to be a metallurgist, estimated that the structure was at least 200 years old. Edward confirmed to us that we are actually 210 years into the future. We saw that New York City had been totally destroyed, and continued to steam south to see if we could determine if life existed. We obtained an old newspaper that was in readable condition in Atlantic City, New Jersey. The headline shouted about the breakdown of nuclear arms talks between Iran and the United States. It was dated April 12, 2018. So we figured that was the date the war broke out, less than a year *after* we had set sail. Then we encountered Edward and Margaret, and you know the rest. So please tell us about yourself and this place, Bill. We were expecting the Wizard of Oz, not that you'd know about that, but instead we find you. If you don't mind me saying, Bill, you seem like a neighbor down the block, not some person from 210 years into our future."

He laughed so hard I thought he's faint.

"Of course I know about the Wizard of Oz!" Bill said. "Judy Garland, Burt Lahr, Jack Haley, and Ray Bolger. One of my favorite movies—even though it's 388 years old."

Another laugh. If nothing else, this guy is likeable, I thought.

"So, you asked who I am and who are we. Fair questions, and I'll do my best to answer them. You've met me, Bill Wellfleet—or *The Samah*, if you're into bullshit. Sorry, but I believe that's the way you'd say it in 2017."

Now it was our turn to laugh. Here's a guy from 210 years into the future, and he speaks perfect idiomatic English, including cusswords, as if we were in 2017.

"Folks," Jack said, "I'd like to make a suggestion if it's okay with Bill. Rather than the three of us telling the department heads and the crew about what we hear today, could we make a video of our meeting?"

"Sure," Bill said. "We have great video recording equipment here."

He made a call from a house phone and a guy walked in with a video camera on a tripod.

"This is Bill Wellfleet," he said into the camera. "I'm here at the Greenbrier with our guests, Admiral Ashley Patterson, Lieutenant Jack Thurber, and Father Rick Sampson, all from the American aircraft carrier, *the USS Ronald Reagan*. I'm about to explain the Greenbrier, and what we do."

He looked at me and I gave him a thumbs up. He returned the gesture. Even hand signals from our time are still used here, I thought.

"We have one mission in life," Bill Wellfleet said, "and that's to preserve the remnants of civilization, the civilization that came crashing down on April 12, 2018. Shortly I'm going to show you how we do that, but for now, please understand our mission."

"Do you folks have a name, like the Greenbrier Gang or something?" asked Father Rick.

"Great name!" said Bill, laughing as usual. "Too bad we didn't think of that. We call ourselves *The Keepers* for short. It's short for *The Keepers of Time*. It's our mission to make sure that history doesn't start over with every new birth. Think of us as a group—a pretty large group—of historians. Yes, we're historians, every one of us. You've met Edward and Margaret. They're typical *Keepers*; they know history."

"Bill," I said, "please tell us about the political situation. We understand the United States no longer exists. How are people governed? Is there any government at all?"

"Yes, we actually have a government," Bill said, "although it may look somewhat different from what you're used to. If you studied us, you may conclude that I'm a dictator, which is anything but true. I came into my position by proclamation, but there wasn't any organized voting. I took power just like my ancestors did, by agreement, if not by actual vote. As a student of history that I am, I've learned that democracy, especially a republican form of democracy as you had in the United States, is the best form of government. So although I was given a lot of power, I immediately gave a lot back, just like all of my predecessors. We have a voting board and by-laws that enables future boards to vote themselves into office, not by an edict from the boss. I've put in place people who keep me in *my* place. What used to be called the United States is now just a vast region of groups of people who live in towns. That's what we call them, *towns,* even though they are not political entities. The primary form of government is determined by warlords. Yes, warlords, petty dictators who rule by whim. The region—I can no longer call it a country—is more like feudal Japan than anything resembling what America once was. But here at the Greenbrier we do have a functioning government. We have laws and law enforcement, and we have a court system. We actually have an infrastructure, with garbage collection and electrical maintenance. We have all of this stuff because we read the history of how a society can and should be run. But most of current-day society in the towns, and especially the leadership, never got the memo, as you folks like to say. We also have a strong military, as you may have noticed when you landed. But in our case, the military is for defense, not raids on neighboring towns, which is what the warlords use their military for."

"How big is the area controlled by *The Keepers?*" Jack asked.

"We cover a large area, well, large being a relative term. We're about the size that Manhattan once was, 34 square miles. There are other enclaves of *The Keepers,* which I'll tell you about shortly."

"When did this all start?" I asked. "Right after the nuclear war, or the *Big War* as we've been calling it?"

"No, a few years before then. Did you notice the inscription on the front of this building that said, 'Ezekiel Hall'?"

"Yes, I meant to ask you about that," I said.

"It's named after the man who started all of this, the man who founded *The Keepers*, although he didn't call us that originally. He was Ezekiel Wellfleet, my distant grandfather. Grandpa Zeke, as we call him, is best described as an eccentric. He was a survivalist, the kind of person who built fallout shelters and stored a lot of bottled water and canned food. You would probably refer to him as a nut-job. A popular genre of fiction in your day concerned 'preppers,' eccentric people like Grandpa Zeke who spent a lot of time prepping or preparing for the worst. Well, crazy as he may have been, Grandpa Zeke is responsible for the remnants of American civilization that you see, God bless him. Turns out, he was right. Nuclear war and all of its devastation was not just a theoretical possibility, it actually happened— 210 years ago. At Grandpa Zeke's direction, the Greenbrier was ready for the war. We have a 250,000-gallon diesel fuel storage tank, which can run our series of electrical generators as backup to our solar panels and windmills. Grandpa Zeke was a very wealthy man, as many eccentrics are. He bought the Greenbrier in 2008, and actually ran it profitably as a resort, but his goal was not being an innkeeper. He was interested in the gigantic bunker that is part of this building. As I believe you know, the U.S. Government kept a nuclear fortified bunker as a place to house the government in case of a disaster. The government abandoned the project in 1995 after a newspaper article divulged its secrecy. No sense having a secret location that's not a secret. Well, the disaster occurred, and thanks to Grandpa Zeke, we're sitting on top of a repository of civilization.

"The facility includes five theaters, run by a theater manager. You can see any movie ever produced as well as every TV show that ever aired. You can also listen to every radio broadcast that's ever been heard, including Orson Wells' famous *War of the Worlds*."

"How did he manage to do that?" Jack asked.

"Grandpa Zeke was a very persuasive guy, as well as a realist. He convinced every producer of every show to allow him to archive their broadcasts—for a reasonable fee—with the provision that it would be for archival purposes only, and that he would never sell any of the information to compete with the originator of the content."

"Is this anything like the Iron Mountain?" said Father Rick. "I recall that a company named Iron Mountain maintained vast archives of corporate data for a fee."

"Yes," said Bill. "The Iron Mountain facilities still exist, including a depleted ore mine under 100 acres in Livingston, New York, a former missile storage battery in Massachusetts, and a former limestone mine in Pennsylvania. It was a vast operation of records archiving and management."

"So whatever became of Iron Mountain as a company?" Father Rick asked.

"The Iron Mountain facilities are alive and well, and all of them are now proud parts of *The Keepers of Time,*" said Bill. "We have a huge network of sites, but, I must say, none as elegant as The Greenbrier. Hey, why don't I take you folks on a trip to the past?"

Bill led us to a door, a 25-ton blast door, and we entered a bunker that was built 720 feet into a hillside. A guy trailed us with the videocam on his shoulder. We were about to see the results of Grandpa Zeke's passion. When we emerged into a large room, Bill turned to face us. He looked like a tour guide who couldn't wait to show us his stuff.

"Welcome to *The Bunker of Time,*" Bill said. "When it was completed in 1961, this space measured 112,544 square feet. Over the years, *The Keepers* have expanded it by more than 20,000 square feet to its present 132,000. Here is where we preserve the past and the present as our gift to the future."

I looked at one wall, about 200 feet long and 30 feet high. The wall consisted of more personal computers than I could have ever imagined in one place. All this and no Internet, I thought.

"The Bunker has four entrances, including one from the main building that we just came through. Its 18 dormitories can hold 1,100 people, but after a recent construction project that will be finished next year, we'll be able to accommodate 2,500. We have purification equipment and three 25,000-gallon water storage tanks. I mentioned that we also have on-site a 250,000-gallon diesel fuel storage tank. Yes, if you're wondering, we own a refinery in Pennsylvania from which we get our fuel. We've built a pipeline to deliver the fuel here A large percentage of our energy comes from solar and wind power. A vast array of solar panels are located a couple of miles from here, next to a 100 acre wind farm, driven by 75 large windmills. We use diesel fuel to fire our generators when wind and solar are insufficient. We have a hospital, including an intensive care unit. There's a large cafeteria, a few smaller dining rooms, and more meeting rooms than I can remember. As you can see from the enormous number of computers, crazy Grandpa Zeke knew that preserving the past meant preserving the digital past. Yes, all of the computers that you see are vintage pre-2018, prewar. But they are all kept in perfect working order by a team of technicians."

"Can you tell us anything about the Internet?" Father Rick said. "In the 21st Century the Internet was a vast electronic organism of interconnected computers. Researching a question meant using an amazing company called Google, which took you to an accurate answer with a few keystrokes. Microsoft's Bing was another option. Communicating meant a thing called email, a way that you could send someone a message anywhere in the world and it would arrive on their computer screen within seconds."

"You just gave an excellent summary of what the Internet was, Father," Bill said. "I have good news for you. The Internet is alive and well, although not nearly as widespread as it was 210 years ago. It is now really an Intranet, for use by *The Keepers* and our colleagues and clients. Grandpa Zeke had the foresight to download enormous amounts of website content to storage devices right here. Yes, we still use the word Google and its wonderful technology. That's how we were able to research you folks and the *USS Ronald Reagan* so quickly. Over the years, we connected to other enclaves of our fellow *Keepers* with thousands of miles of fiber-optic cable. The only thing that's missing is satellite technology, although China has launched a few satellites over the years. There are only about only 100 satellites above the earth, and China isn't sharing them with anyone."

"And how do you communicate?" I said.

"Radio is our primary source of communication, although we use email on our Intranet," Bill said. "Radio is one of the few technologies that still works well. Did you notice the tall metal tower just east of the building? That's a radio tower. With radio, we can contact anyone who has a receiver. We can maintain regular contact with the *Reagan*. Oh, yes, we use encryption technology, so our radio communications are secure."

"Bill," I said, "with a region dominated by warlords as you describe them, do you worry about being attacked?"

"We don't worry, admiral, we prepare. I told you about our well-armed military. We also have a strong air defense system. Yes, there are airplanes, although nowhere nearly as many as the time you people came from."

"What about the events that occurred post *Big War*?" Jack said. I could almost see his journalist's antennas sprouting.

"Come this way, folks," said Bill. "I'm about to show you post-war journalism at its finest."

He escorted us into another large room, attached to another one of equal size.

"Grandpa Wellfleet had the foresight to realize that he needed to put in place a group of people who would record history going forward in the event of a world-wide disaster. In front of you are dozens of the finest journalists you'll ever meet. We even have a school that was organized over 150 years ago to teach the skills and rules of journalism. Lieutenant Jack, I know that you won the Pulitzer Prize. You may want to come back here and spend some time with these folks. You can learn from one another. In this room, and the one adjacent to it, we record what's going on in the world. It's a challenge because the Internet isn't as pervasive as it once was, but these folks rely on every tool available to them to make a record. Somebody once said that 'Journalism is the first rough draft of history.' Well here is where it starts. We even have our own newspaper, known among thoughtful people as the most authoritative in the world. It's called *The Daily Keeper,* and it's published right here."

"Is there any group that you consider your most serious enemy?" I asked.

"Yes, indeed, admiral," said Bill. "A group that calls itself the Eastern Empire is located not too far away in what was once known as Arlington, Virginia. We estimate that they have approximately 10,000 troops under arms. It's headed by a megalomaniacal warlord named Nigel Portland, who calls himself a 'general.' They sustain themselves by raiding encampments of innocent people. They tried to attack us about four years ago. Our superior weapons and well trained soldiers held them off. As I've said before, our strong military is for defensive purposes. But sometimes I think that an offensive against the Army of the Eastern Empire may be a strategic use of defensive doctrine."

He looked me straight in the eyes when he said that. It didn't take too much imagination to figure out what he just said. It seems apparent that this guy wants us on his side. Oh shit, I thought. Here we go again. But then it occurred to me: never change the past is a basic theme of time travel philosophy. But we're not in the past. We're in the future. It looks like I'm going to be spending a lot of time with my advisors, Jack and Father Rick. But for the time being, it looks like the United States (meaning the *USS Ronald Reagan* and its crew) is the best, if not the only ally, that *The Keepers* have.

"Bill," said Jack, "you said that there aren't many aircraft flying around in the year 2227. Why is that? I'm sure that countless planes must have survived the nuclear war. Isn't it a simple question of maintenance, for you as well as any other organized group?"

"Jack," Bill said, "you have just touched upon the greatest problem that has plagued society in the past 210 years—lack of infrastructure, which is caused by a lack of organized government. No organized government means an absence of uniform laws and courts to enforce the law. Without dependable law to govern transactions, conducting business is a nightmare, as any business in a dictatorship knew in your time. The only reliable law was corruption, including bribery. Over the years, finding replacement parts for old aircraft became almost impossible because an industrial base doesn't exist to manufacture them, and there's certainly no reliable widespread infrastructure. There is no central government, and certainly no system of free enterprise to keep the parts flowing. When a plane breaks down, it's broken forever. We're the most organized of all of the groups in the region, but we have as difficult a time as anyone maintaining legacy equipment such as planes."

⟰ ⟱

"Bill," Father Rick said. "Could you please tell us more about these towns that are led by warlords? Would you describe them as amoral, as uncivilized?"

"Yes, Father," said Bill. "Uncivilized and amoral, and more often *immoral* are apt terms to use. Their existence is sustained by plunder and pillage. Their idea of morality is to take prisoners as slaves. They also have depraved forms of entertainment that will disgust you."

"What forms of entertainment?" said Jack.

"Let me show you. But be prepared to be shocked."

With a remote he clicked on a wide screen TV and called up a video from the computer's hard drive. He motioned to the guy with the videocam to aim his camera at the screen so he could record it for the video.

"What you are about to see was recorded by one of our drones just three days ago."

We could see in the distance something that looked like a large stadium. As the drone flew closer and zoomed in, we could see that it actually was a stadium.

"Look familiar?" said Bill.

"Yeah," I said. "It looks like a soccer or football stadium. But I don't see any goalposts. Also I don't see any lines on the ground, just what looks like sand."

The drone panned in on one side of the interior of the stadium. A door opened, and four trumpet players took positions outside the door. Because the drone engine was relatively quiet, we could hear the sounds of the trumpets. A pretty young woman with jet black hair walked through the cortege of trumpeters. She couldn't have been more that 20 or 21. She wore what appeared to be some sort of armored vest. I noticed that she carried a long sword. The drone next focused on the opposite side of the stadium. Another door opened, and out poured the trumpeters. Another pretty young woman appeared. She was tall and slender and had short blond hair. She also wore a vest and carried a sword. The roar of the crowd drowned out the sound of the trumpets. It suddenly dawned on me what was happening. I felt sick, literally, as if I was about to throw up. We were watching the beginning of a gladiatorial fight.

The girls approached each other, sparring and parrying with their swords. The blond swung her sword at the other girl's right arm. A spray of blood arced to the sand. The wounded girl swung her sword back, then arced it down and across, inflicting a long gash in the blond girl's right leg. Another spurt of blood hit the sand. The blond fell to her knees and then staggered to get up, hobbled by her leg injury. The blond swung her sword at the other girl's torso, striking her armored plate. She again fell to her knees, her leg wound gushing blood. The black haired girl swung her sword high and brought it down, sweeping in an arc to the left, decapitating the pretty blond girl. The blood plumed into the air, and, as her headless body fell, a final gush of blood darkened the sand. The crowd screamed so loud, Bill had to lower the volume.

"I gotta use the head," I said, as I ran for the bathroom door. I barfed until I didn't think there was anything left in me. My God, I thought, we're over 200 years into the future but civilization has gone backwards.

When I walked back into the room, I saw Bill, weeping gently and dabbing tears from his face. Jack sat at a table, his head on his arms. Father Rick sat, his hands folded and his eyes closed in prayer.

"I believe you were asking me what kind of civilization exists in *the towns*, Father Rick," Bill said. "You've just seen a perfect example of what the world has become in the last 210 years. The young blond woman you just saw killed was kidnapped from us two years ago. Her name was Nancy Morton. She was a talented computer programmer, one of our best. Along with her they kidnapped her two-year-old daughter, Amy. I'm sure they used their standard procedure to get civilized young people to kill one another. They held her little daughter hostage. If Nancy didn't fight, they would simply kill her daughter, and then use Nancy as wolf bait for another type of exhibition."

I felt like I was going to get sick again.

"Admiral Ashley, any thoughts about what we just saw?" said Bill.

"Yes," I said. "I'm a senior naval officer. My job is to act as I've been trained and not to follow emotions."

I cleared my throat and blew my nose.

"That said," I spoke softly, "I want to destroy that stadium. I *will* destroy that stadium, along with the vermin who created it, and I don't give a flying fuck what year we're in."

I was definitely having a hard time with my anti-profanity rule.

"I think we could all use a break," Bill Wellfleet said. "Let's get back together here in 20 minutes and we'll have lunch, if you still have an appetite after what we just saw."

I pulled Jack close to me.

"Let's not forget our mission, Jack. We have to learn everything possible about the run up to the war and its aftermath. That's the information I'll need to give our government when we get back."

⇥ ⇤

After lunch we entered one of the smaller theaters, with a capacity of about 100 people, more than enough for our small group.

"Bill," I said, "you've given us a fascinating review of the *Keepers* and what you're all about. But I need to know more about the war, how it began, and how it changed society."

Besides Bill, there were a couple of other people I hadn't met. Bill introduced Wesley Drummond, a psychologist as well as an historian (all of *The Keepers* are historians), and Madeline Fornier, a linguist.

"Folks," said Bill Wellfleet, "we've been bombarding you with bits and pieces of information and you've done likewise. We decided that it was best to give you a top down history of what's happened in the past 200 or more years, and it will center on the nuclear war as Admiral Ashley requested. The camera is rolling so you can bring this all back to share with your staff on the ship. But first, do any of you folks have any comments about your impressions of what you've seen already."

"Yes, Bill," I said. "If there's one thing that all of us have noticed it's that you people seem to be from our time. You look, talk, and

77

even dress like we did back in 2017. Your speech patterns even include colloquialisms that we use, even slang and vulgarities. We expected to find people wearing futuristic clothing, not that I know what that means. But you guys could walk down any street in America and nobody would ever notice.

"Admiral, your question goes to the very essence of what happened after the *Big War,* and the very essence of what happened in the years immediately afterward. As *The Keepers of Time,* we did and still do, just that. We have records from the years after the war. It took over five years for the radioactive levels to stabilize in some places, but members of *The Keepers,* using radiation detectors, began to fan out looking for written memoirs of what happened. Some people, quite a few actually, kept extensive diaries of the post-war days. Those diaries have become an important part of our knowledge of the lost world. The early *Keepers,* the original ones, developed a strong belief that our culture should closely resemble the one that was lost. Here at the Greenbrier, there was no physical impact from the nuclear war at all. Grandpa Zeke knew what he was doing. So that's why our manner of dress and speech looks so familiar to you. We intend to keep it that way, because of our commitment to preservation. What I just said applies to *The Keepers,* both here at the Greenbrier, and at our other locations. It most emphatically does *not* apply to the rest of the world as we know it. I'm going to ask Wes Drummond, our head psychologist, to explain further."

Drummond stood to speak. He was medium height, maybe 5'10" and had a wiry build, with long brown hair. I figured he was around 45.

"The war changed everything," Drummond said. "Ever since the war, people have wondered what would become of society. *The Keepers,* on the other hand, have a clearly defined mission. You may wonder why Bill asked a psychologist to speak to you. The reason I'm standing in front of you is to explain that the world, or to be more specific, America, has undergone a shift in its way of thinking in the past 200 years. You folks tell us that we seem like you. Yes, we are like you. We think of ourselves as people from the 21st Century. We have our beliefs and our morals. We agree on countless things that make society work. We think that stealing is bad, unjustified killing and violence are bad. If we see someone who needs help, we ask what we can do. I'm not suggesting that the 21st Century was a panacea of virtue. From our reading of history we noticed some bizarre behaviors. But now it's become a spectacle of two people killing each other in gladiatorial games. Besides the anti-social behavior, we've studied that a huge shift has occurred in the attitude of groups toward one another. There's a lack of cooperation, a lack of trust. That's why we haven't seen the formation of a central well-intentioned government. It almost happened once, about 100 years ago, but it was a short-lived experiment. A group of 10 towns actually banded together and elected a representative form of government. That lasted for about five years, and then collapsed into anarchy. Yes, we see some elements of cooperation, but it's usually at the individual level, between two people looking for a mutual benefit. One person will provide extra food to another in exchange for a couple of gladiatorial tickets. If there's one word that best describes most of what used to be America, it's moral depravity."

"Why do you see the lack of cooperation and trust, not to mention the depravity?" Jack asked.

"The answer is as simple as it is complicated. In this age, very few people care about history. They see no need for it, and can't understand why anyone would care. A key indicator of mental health is the ability to postpone gratification. There's little or none of that in the towns. They live for the present, with no thoughts of the past or future."

"Mr. Drummond," I said, "of all of these towns we've heard of, are you telling us that none of them show any trust or cooperation?"

"That's a great question," Drummond said, "and the answer, happily, is yes, there are pockets of normal human relations. *The Keepers* have excellent relations with seven towns. We provide them with access to our vast database as well as technical assistance with their equipment, and we exchange raw materials and food. We actually have an active trading relationship with those towns, based on mutual cooperation and trust. But they are only seven towns out of several hundred, not counting the other *Keepers* facilities, of course."

I raised my hand. I wanted to make sure that a lot of questions got answered, not just for us, but for the people on the *Reagan* who would see this video.

"Mr. Drummond," I said, "the most jolting thing I've seen since the rubble of New York City was a gladiatorial fight between two pretty young women. It literally sickened me, as the others can tell you. I had to run to the bathroom. You used the word 'depravity.' Can you explain to us what those disgusting contests are all about?"

"Certainly, admiral," said Drummond. "In your time, which is the time that *The Keepers* have adopted, athletic competition was a wonderful thing. I think you've seen our soccer stadium, and if not you should. In your time, baseball, basketball, football, and soccer, were the popular sports in America. Post-war, the psychology of people, most people, has changed and it's changed for the worse. Gladiatorial contests took hold about 75 years ago. A form of recreation that we thought died with ancient Rome, has reared its vicious head. It's the most popular spectator sport in what used to be America. The participants are typically slaves, except for a few psychopaths who indulge in the fights out of their own desire to kill. The slaves, as I know Bill has explained to you, are kidnapped from other towns after raids. Family members of the slaves are held hostage. It's either fight and kill or watch your loved one get killed. Every town has a stadium or at least an amphitheater, a place where people kill one another for sport. Yes, I used the word depraved, because I can think of no other way to describe it."

"What can you do about it?" Father Rick asked.

"Bill can answer that question better than I can, but I know he'll agree when I say that we do what we've been doing for over 200 years. We maintain a strong defense. It's rare that one of the lawless towns attacks a *Keepers* facility. That's for two reasons. First, our main product is knowledge and information, things that the warlords and their followers aren't interested in. The second reason is that we maintain enough military power to repel an invasion."

"But the towns have drones or at least some of them do," Jack said. "How do you maintain security from overhead surveillance?"

"Our forces and our hardware are constantly on the move," Drummond said, "I won't go into more detail than that. We're not stupid, as our adversaries have learned, certainly not as stupid as them. We also have a powerful anti-aircraft defense system."

$$\Longleftarrow \Longrightarrow$$

"Ashley, it's Commander Blakely, the XO, for you He says it's urgent." Jack handed me the radio.

"Admiral," Blakely said, "we've spotted a drone aircraft five miles out and closing on our position. I've launched a Hornet to intercept if necessary."

"Bill," I said, turning to Wellfleet, "do you have any drones operating off the coast of Baltimore?"

"No, admiral. I'm sure it's from the Eastern Empire. Besides us, they're the only people around here who have a drone fleet."

"Shoot it down, Mike," I said to my XO.

"Aye aye, ma'am.

"And Mike," I said. "Advise me if you see any other aircraft. Shoot to kill on sight without my authorization."

I glanced at Bill Wellfleet, who looked at me slack-jawed.

"I didn't want to wait and see if the drone was armed," I said. "I have a carrier to protect. Do their drones normally carry missiles?"

"They're mainly used for surveillance, admiral, but sometimes they use rocket fire to support ground troops in a raid."

"I don't know if we're at war or not, but whatever it is, it looks like I just fired the first shot," I said.

⊷⊷ ⊷⊷

"Before we were so rudely interrupted," I said, "I believe you folks were about to tell us about the *Big War.*"

"I'll defer to Bill Wellfleet on the history of the *Big War,* admiral," Drummond said. "Bill is an expert on the subject."

Bill Wellfleet walked toward the podium. He wore khaki trousers, a starched white shirt with no tie, a double-breasted navy blue blazer, and Gucci loafers. Every time I look at one of these *Keepers* people, I think I'm back in 2017. Bill could have been a model for a Brooks Brothers catalog.

"Well, I'm about to discuss the single most important event of the past 210 years. We've given you pieces of information, and a lot of it you already know from your travels, such as New York City. I'm going to concentrate on the run-up to the war, and the first few years after it. The most important word that I can think of, and I've written a book on the subject, is 'underestimate,' as in 'never underestimate the intentions of your enemy.' The second word is 'intelligence.' When you have active intelligence, don't ignore it.

"In the latter days of *PWT* or Pre-war Time, the United States was busy gathering intelligence on the Islamic Republic of Iran. The two nations, and you know this part, had signed a Nuclear Arms Deal in 2015, along with six other countries led by the United States, limiting Iran's ability to enrich uranium to bomb grade in exchange for a gradual releasing of sanctions. Uranium mined from the earth is less than 1 percent U-235, the isotope used to fuel reactors and make bombs. Centrifuges are needed to separate the U-235 from the other part of the uranium, in a process called enrichment. The other fuel that can be used to make a bomb, plutonium, is made by irradiating uranium in a nuclear reactor. The process transforms some of the uranium into plutonium. During enrichment, centrifuges were used to raise concentrations of U-235. For most power reactors, uranium is enriched up to 5 percent. Bomb grade is above 90 percent and Iran had been processing uranium ore to a 20 percent enrichment level, or so the American government thought. The whole objective, from the West's point of view, was to limit Iran's ability to make bombs. The way to achieve that objective, the United States believed, was careful inspections and monitoring."

"The agreement called for some pretty strict limits on centrifuges, if I recall," Jack said. "From what you're saying, Iran simply ignored the limits?"

"Yes, the huge uranium plant at Natanz was limited to five thousand centrifuges, about half of its pre-agreement level. In the year after the agreement, the United States complained of numerous violations of the agreement by Iran. An Iranian scientist who survived the war documented that Iran used its plant at Natanz as a waving flag. The thinking of the Mullahs was that if you keep the Americans busy with numerous small violations, it would free Iran for bigger projects, and that's exactly what happened. It had been in planning before, in the two years prior to the signing of the agreement. The Iranians had a well-known reputation in the West for duplicity, of out-and-out lying. Israeli Prime Minister, Benjamin Netanyahu, called the agreement a 'historic mistake,' one that would create a 'terrorist nuclear superpower.' Netanyahu proved to be prophetic, although he would perish in less than three years. What Iran managed to pull off was the most historic ruse in the history of man. While the United

States and its allies busied themselves with inspections at Natanz, Iran was creating an even bigger facility right nearby, about twice the size of Natanz. The uranium enrichment went unobstructed. By then, the centrifuges spun at a 90 percent enrichment level— the bomb making level. Unknown to American intelligence, Iran and North Korea had begun a process of cooperation that would bring the world as it then existed to an end. North Korea, while millions of its citizens suffered from malnutrition, managed to buy 50 nuclear weapons on the black market that resulted after the fall of the Soviet Union, and then obtained another 85 nukes from Iran.

"The second part of the great ruse involved delivery of the bombs," Bill continued. "The West assumed that without intercontinental ballistic missiles, ICBMs, a hostile power would be limited to suitcase nuclear bombs. Both Iran and North Korea realized that there was a much easier way to deliver a large number of nuclear weapons. The answer was short-range ballistic missiles, or SRBMs, which could be carried on freighters and tankers. Both countries delivered their weapons on commercial ships sailing under various flags. North Korea came to an end in the exchange that followed, attacked by the United States, with an assist from South Korea. China decided to look the other way."

The radio sounded. Jack handed it to me.

"Admiral, Mike Blakely again. I'm calling to inform you that we were approached by two other drones. Our Hornet pilot identified them both as Predator drones. Both have been attacked and destroyed. I''ll let you know of any other developments, ma'am."

"Very well, Mike. Keep me informed."

"Bill," I said, "Sorry, but we had to take care of business."

"Your response time to a threat is impressive, admiral," Bill said, shaking his head.

"I shoot first because there may be no time to ask questions later. Before that radio call, Bill, I was about to ask you what happened to the rest of the world," I said.

"It was definitely a World War, admiral. London was totally devastated, as well as Paris, Rome, Madrid, and Berlin.

"Although once protected by its vast spaces, Russia lost its central government and returned to a pre-czarist state. It's now controlled by small units, similar to *the towns* in what used to be America. The United States retaliated against Middle Eastern countries, helped by Russia to its ability. The Iranians got the 'end of days' conflagration they were looking for. The capital city, Tehran, was destroyed, as well as the Holy City of Qum, and Kharg Island. The country is no longer a state but a lawless region similar to the tribal times of the Dark Ages. They use the ancient name to refer to what's left—Persia. Before the breakdown in the compliance talks, American intelligence suspicions had also focused on Syria, of course, and then on Libya, both strongholds of that barbaric group called the Islamic State or ISIS. The retaliation against those countries was also massive. One could argue that Israel got lucky. Only one bomb hit the country in a relatively unpopulated area. Historians have identified navigational errors as the reason that Israel was spared. But Israel was by then a sole outpost of civilization in a lawless region, an outpost without the friendship of its protector, the United States."

"So was any country or countries left standing?" said Jack.

"Yes, Jack," said Wellfleet, "China, Japan, and South Korea, now simply known as Korea, survived and prosper—well that's a relative term—to this day. If there's any such thing as a super power, it's definitely China. Within 10 years after the war, China abandoned communism entirely, and is an active trading partner of all of the countries of Asia. Oh yes, I should add, Taiwan is now part of China. They reunited after Taiwan realized that the old animosities caused by communism no longer existed."

"Are any of these countries active in what used to be America?" said Father Rick.

"It depends on what you call 'active,' " said Wellfleet. "For the first 10 years after the war, they apparently ignored the West. The ruling policy over 200 years appears to be that the West and the Middle East created the problem that led to the war, so now they must live with it. But *The Keepers of Time* have a very good relationship with China and the other countries of Asia. I will never forget the day, 15 years ago, when a gentleman named Mi-Ki Chun appeared on the doorstep of the Greenbrier. We call him 'Mickey,' and communicate with him regularly. The purpose of his visit, on behalf of the government of China, was to inquire if they might have access to some of our vast database of knowledge. I'll never forget his reaction when I said 'Sure, what would you be willing to pay for our services?' Without batting an eye, Mickey said $10 Million in the equivalent of the old American dollar. Inflation has hardly existed since the *Big War,* so $10 million was a wonderful sum. Mickey couldn't believe that we were willing to share our database. I didn't want him to renege on his offer, so I didn't explain to him that our mission is to disseminate history, not keep it hidden. We're hooked up via an old cross-Pacific fiber optic cable connected to land lines that still exist. It did require some trenching on land, but China was happy to foot the cost. I know you will want to ask this question, whether China has launched any satellites. The answer is yes. They have about 100 satellites in space. China is the only country with rocket technology to enable a space launch. I think that soon they'll see no risk in opening satellite access to the world. Soon, the old Internet will be resurrected, and worldwide communications will be back to where it was—210 years ago."

"Whatever became of radical Islam? Does it still exist?" asked Father Rick.

"The religion of Islam still exists," Wellfleet said, "but what was known as radical Islam died on the vine after the war, or rather it was killed. In the lawlessness that existed in the few years post-war, worldwide rage centered on radical Islam. Muslims, even quiet, peaceful Muslims, were hunted down and killed. Mosques were destroyed, and virtually any vestige of the radical elements were dead. But the horrors of the radical fringes of Islam lived on, although in a secular way. The barbarians who created the towns adopted the worst parts of the once hated Islamic fringe. The gladiatorial stadiums, when not in use for fighting, are used for spectacles of death by stoning. Yes, believe it or not, stoning to death still exists. We didn't show you a drone video taken recently at the Eastern Empire stadium because we felt it would be too upsetting. It showed a young woman, buried in sand up to her shoulders, being stoned to death by an enthusiastic gang of 12 men, as the crowd in the stadium cheered them on. It took her 15 minutes before she stopped moving. Then one of the men walked up to her pit and hurled a large rock at her head, finishing her off. The offense for which she was killed? Adultery. Her 78-year-old assigned husband accused her of sneaking off with a young man. The accused young man was stoned to death the following morning. Morning was chosen because gladiatorial fights were scheduled for that afternoon. Besides death by stoning, the town barbarians have also adopted the old radical Islamic punishments of cutting off the limb of a person accused of stealing. So yes, radical Islam is dead, but the reasons people hated and feared it live on."

"We looked long and far for evidence of human beings before we finally came upon you folks," I said. "What is the current population of the world, if you have any idea?"

"Admiral, prepare to be shocked," said Bill. "In the year you came from, the world population was estimated to be 7.3 billion people, with 326 million in the United States. Now, and of course the figures are far from exact, we estimate the population of the world to be 900 million, with the former United States at 25 million. The world has shrunk in the past 210 years."

"My God," I said, "is that because of the *Big War?*"

"Yes," said Wellfleet, "either directly or from its consequences over the past two centuries. The mass devastation of the bombings caused millions of deaths. Over the next five years many millions succumbed to radiation poisoning, and cancer deaths from radioactivity continued for decades. But there was, and *is*, an even bigger problem: fertility. Genetic mutations resulting from the worldwide fallout over the years caused changes in the ability of most women to reproduce. It began in the years after the war, and has accelerated every year.

"I know you all laughed when we walked the grounds here this morning, and people stopped and applauded as a young pregnant woman walked down the path. I applauded too. It's a wonderful sight, and a rare one. The fertility rate worldwide simply isn't anywhere near the replacement level. That fact only adds to the insanity of the towns' sacrificing the lives of young people of child-rearing age in the arena, people who just may have been fertile. I hope I'm not being overdramatic when I say that the human race could be facing extinction."

"Bill, thank you for your hospitality, and especially for your history lesson," I said. "I don't think any of us are too happy with what you had to say, but reality doesn't arrange itself to please us. I'm going to address my senior staff before we show them this video to prepare them for the shock. I'm going to hold off showing it to the crew as long as possible. Aboard ship, morale is always an issue."

CHAPTER THIRTEEN

"Good morning, ladies and gentlemen, this is Shepard Smith reporting for Fox News. A gigantic story has just burst into our newsroom. The *USS Ronald Reagan*, a Nimitz Class nuclear aircraft carrier, has apparently disappeared. The *Reagan* was steaming off the coast of Eastern Long Island, along with three other ships in Carrier Strike Group 2311, when, according to eyewitnesses, she was gone. There have been no reports of an explosion, and nobody who's been interviewed reported seeing the ship sink. She's simply gone. The other ships in the strike group are unharmed and very much afloat."

As Smith spoke, the program ran stock video footage of the *USS Ronald Reagan*, steaming alongside smaller ships.

"Carrier Strike Group 2311, with the *Reagan* as the flagship, was headed toward Boston for a brief stop before deploying to the Persian Gulf. The ship had just spent a few days in New York City for Fleet Week. The *Reagan* is a large ship, almost 1,100 feet in length.

She carries 3,200 people in the ship's company, and 2,480 in its air wing. We called the Office of Naval Operations. They're normally very helpful folks, but they have nothing to give us right now.

"The waters off Long island, where the *Reagan* disappeared, are not very deep. Sources that we've contacted have told us that the depth where the *Reagan* was last seen is no more than 150 feet.

"At this point folks, until we learn more, it's a mystery, a 101,000-ton mystery.

Needless to say, Fox News going to follow this story carefully throughout the day, and we'll keep you up to the minute as we receive any additional reports."

The *Reagan* had been missing for 10 minutes.

⇒+ +⇐

Day Seven

We stayed overnight, courtesy of *The Samah*, Bill Wellfleet. Breakfast was served in the main lobby. I hardly ate a thing, my stomach still wrenching from the horrible scene of the young gladiatrixes the afternoon before. We planned to take Bill Wellfleet with us back to the *Reagan* after we finished breakfast.

A tall, thin, elegant woman entered the room. She was about 5'11" with dark hair mixed with specks of gray. I figured she was in her early 40s. She wore a khaki outfit of pants, a blouse, and a photographer's vest. Could there be an Abercrombie & Fitch outlet nearby? I thought.

"William, dahling, are you keeping our new friends to yourself?"

Something told me that this 23rd Century lady spent a lot of time watching old movies. She seemed to be channeling Lauren Bacall, and she pulled it off beautifully.

"Magda, please join us," said Bill as he jumped up and walked over to give the woman a hug.

"Folks, let me introduce my wife, Magda. She's been away inspecting one of our other facilities."

Magda, with the studied elegance of the silver screen, walked up to each of us and gave a gracious, warm handshake. She gave me a kiss on the cheek.

"Among her many chores," said Bill, "Magda is the director of our theater company, the *Keepers of the Stage*. She's a wonderful actress and a terrific administrator."

"Please don't think of me as a phony, dahlings," said Magda, "but I find that acting out a role is an improvement on reality. Edward and Margaret have brought me up to date on you folks. I hope Bill feels as honored as I do to have you with us. I understand that you have come to us from the distant past, 2017 if I recall Edward saying. We *Keepers* know about this thing called time travel, although we haven't experienced it. It's so exciting to have you with us, visitors from a time before the *Big War*. I trust that my husband has shown you the wonderful innards of *The Bunker*. As I'm sure you've noticed, we *Keepers* tend to dress and talk as if it were 210 years ago. We find that the past has many attractions that the present lacks."

"Magda," I said, "We're about to show Bill the *USS Ronald Reagan*. I'd be happy to have you join us and see life in 2017."

"I'd be ecstatic, madam admiral, simply ecstatic. But can I ask you to stay one more evening as my special guests. We're putting on our production of *The Sound of Music* in the main theater tonight, and I'd love to have you all as my guests of honor."

That evening, we walked into what Magda referred to as the main theater. I was stunned by the beauty of the place. Jack and Father Rick agreed with me that it looked like Carnegie Hall. The aisles were elegantly appointed by footlights, and the stage curtains were a deep violet. The 18 members of the orchestra sat in the pit tuning their instruments. The conductor, *wearing a tuxedo,* a man named Sydney Morland, looked our way and bowed graciously. *The Sound of Music* was always one of my favorite plays. The production was a challenge for the orchestra as well as the actors with singing roles, because the Rogers and Hammerstein score was such a part of our culture and the script demanded that it be done right. The last time I saw the play was a high school production in which my niece had a role. Even with high school kids and amateur music, it was a joy. The beautiful story of the von Trapp family as they made their journey of escape from Nazi occupied Austria is one of the thrills of the stage. The theater was almost full. Apparently the citizens of the Greenbrier enjoyed Magda's productions.

Bill Wellfleet walked up to the microphone, extended his hand in our direction, and said "Ladies and gentlemen, let's give a Greenbrier welcome to our guests from the sea." The crowd applauded warmly.

The orchestra began playing before the curtains opened. Magda walked to center stage. She played the lead of Maria von Trapp, the role made famous by Julie Andrews. Maria was the woman who took a job as the family governess and then fell in love with the handsome widower, Captain von Trapp. She sang the title song, "The Hills are Alive with the Sound of Music," accompanied by the Rogers and Hammerstein score. I felt tears well up in my eyes. I looked at Jack, and then Father Rick, who said, "West Virginia? This is Broadway."

Magda had an angelic voice and a powerful one. We would later agree that she was at least as good as Julie Andrews, maybe even better.

We sat through the most wonderful evening of music and song that I can remember. When it ended we all wiped tears from our eyes. It was a pleasant way for us to forget, temporarily, our strange circumstances in another time.

Bill insisted that we attend the cast party in the main lobby after the performance. Since we weren't heading back to the ship until the next morning, I agreed. He and Magda walked up to our group, followed by a waiter with a tray of champagne.

"I hope you folks enjoyed your brief time away from your ship," Magda said.

I think we all embarrassed ourselves by gushing over Magda's performance. It didn't feel like we were in a far, dystopian, post-nuclear-war future. We felt at home.

"Bill, Magda, I have an observation," I said. "This evening was the best performance of *The Sound of Music* that I've ever seen." Jack and Father Rick nodded in agreement.

"What strikes me is that just yesterday we saw that sickening gladiatorial fight in one of your neighboring towns. But here, I feel like we're standing in an outpost of civilization."

"When Grandpa Zeke conceived of *The Keepers of Time*," Bill said, "he didn't intend it just as an information storage and retrieval system. He wanted *The Keepers* to be the keepers of culture as well. I think he did a good job."

⇥ ⇤

The next morning we prepared for our flight back to the *Reagan*. I asked Bill to assign help to lift some heavy and bulky electronic gear off the *Sea King*. With two additional people aboard, space was getting tight. We can retrieve the gear at a later date, I thought.

As we walked up to the helicopter, Bill Wellfleet leaned closer to me and said, "Admiral, I think you'll find that the relationship between Magda and I is a lot like you and Lieutenant Jack. We're happily married, still in love, and consider ourselves best friends."

"I had noticed that Bill," I said. "It's good to know that some of the better parts of civilization still exist."

CHAPTER FOURTEEN

A drien Drake inspected his shock troops, the elite members of his army. He wore his usual gray officer's uniform that he had copied from old pre-war Egypt. His chest was adorned with over 75 medals, although he had never seen combat. Actually he had never served in any military unit other than the one he formed, the Army of Cleveland Town. He obtained the medals from an old facility that once housed a US Army base.

Adrien Drake, or General Drake, as he insisted on being called, was the warlord of Cleveland Town, an area that was once part of the City of Cleveland before the *Big War*. His area of control covered approximately 40 square miles. As a careful warrior chief, he had built heavily protected bunkers on the perimeter of the town. It was impossible to enter Cleveland Town without permission, and nobody tried.

He walked up and down the ranks of his 3,000 troops, loudly reprimanding any soldier whose uniform wasn't perfect. One soldier's epaulets were on backwards. He tore them off and threw them to the ground.

After his inspection he would travel five miles to the north to check on the construction of the new stadium. Drake knew, as did all of the warlords, that a key to remaining in power is to keep the population happy, and, if not happy, at least entertained. The cheapest and easiest form of entertainment was gladiatorial games. Young men, and women, who were captured in raids on other towns, provided a steady flow of fighters. They were not always willing killers, but a sure way to gain their enthusiasm was to hold family members hostage. They had a choice of fighting to the death in the arena, or watching their family killed. If they had no family members for hostage, they would be faced with certain death if they refused to fight. Whenever the supply of fighters ran low, there was always the option of wolves, the countless numbers of hungry animals, which would be set loose in the arena against helpless captive slaves.

When completed, the stadium would be named the Rudolph Drake Stadium, in honor of Adrien Drake's great-grandfather, the man who organized Cleveland Town. The stadium was about three months from completion, and when finished, would hold 10,000 spectators, not a huge amount, but enough for the size of Cleveland Town, which had a population of 200,000. To obtain tickets to the events, the citizens had to accumulate points through a complicated system of merits and demerits that also helped to control the work behavior of the population. The people of Cleveland Town drew their income primarily from a network of small manufacturing plants. The town specialized in making small arms. The managers of the three operating plants had long ago learned the art of copying old designs carefully, and the resulting guns were known to be the best, and were available for purchase by other towns.

The point system, through which the citizens could satisfy their bloodlust at the gladiatorial games, worked well with a manufacturing economy. The more completed weapons that a person signed off on, the greater the number of points. The greatest amount of demerits would be assessed whenever a weapon exploded on testing.

Because Cleveland Town's manufacturing output—guns— could also become its greatest security risk, General Drake staffed each plant with a dozen guards, armed not with the locally made handguns, but with still-reliable old M16 automatic machine guns.

The main steel smelting plant for Cleveland Town's gun shops was a large former auto manufacturing facility with a smoke stack that soared 150 feet into the air. The fuel for the plant was coal, brought in ample supplies from various mines across Virginia, West Virginia, and Ohio. A basic article of clothing for the residents of Cleveland Town was a surgical mask to filter out the coal dust.

Cleveland Town enjoyed a steady stream of income from the sale of handguns to other towns, to other warlords. The largest customer was The Eastern Empire. Drake always thought the name, the Eastern Empire, was pretentious. It was really just another town, although a large one. It occupies the area that once comprised Arlington, Virginia and Washington, D.C. But Nigel Portland had more soldiers under arms than any other town, with The Army of the Eastern Empire and its 10,000 troops. Recently, the income of Cleveland Town saw a large drop after Nigel Portland's troops raided an old U.S. Army weapons depot, the Picatinny Arsenal, cutting down on his need for guns from Cleveland. Adrien Drake responded to the problem by dispatching representatives to all of the towns within 1,000 miles of Cleveland Town to hawk their guns.

Blake continued his inspection of the interior of the new stadium. He had directed his chief architect to provide no fewer than six doors that faced inward to the arena floor. After seeing countless gladiatorial contests in other towns, including the big stadium in the Eastern Empire, he concluded that more action was required. So rather than have two opponents enter the arena to face each other alone, his new design would enable pitched battles between groups of gladiators.

"If I close my eyes I can hear the roar of the crowd already," he said to Colonel Jubal Jackson, his chief of staff.

Although the stadium was not yet completed, Drake told his assistant to arrange for a fight between two newly acquired slaves for the enjoyment of their small group.

Two young men, actually teenagers, emerged from doors at opposite ends of the stadium. They walked toward one another, swinging their swords. The boys had been captured only two weeks before, and had just begun their gladiatorial training. During their brief time in captivity, they had become close friends. The taller of the two boys was armed with a short sword and a net. As he and his opponent—his friend—approached one another, the tall boy fell forward with his sword facing up. He killed himself rather than give Drake and his lot the joy of seeing two friends trying to murder each other.

In the interest of time, Drake decided against arranging another gladiatorial contest.

The two men walked down the street to the Cuyahoga River, which ran through Cleveland Town and emptied to the north into Lake Erie. They boarded a 25-foot boat and, with Jackson at the helm, proceeded up the river toward the lake. Drake wanted to inspect the loading facilities at the head of the river, the primary spot where raw supplies entered the town, and from which the Cleveland guns would journey to customers. In old times, before the *Big War*, the Cuyahoga River achieved fame for actually catching on fire from its infusion with oil and industrial waste.

But the old stories of the fiery river didn't impress Drake. By his orders, debris from the town's manufacturing plants still emptied into the river, and began a polluted journey toward Lake Erie.

CHAPTER FIFTEEN

Day Eight

As we approached the *Reagan*, Bill turned to Magda and said, "Just like the old videos we've seen, but even more impressive up close."

We landed on deck and I turned off the engines, giving us all a pleasant silence after our flight.

"Do you think that Admiral Patterson is ready for the *Big Talk*?" Magda whispered into Bill's ear.

He looked at her, smiled, and nodded. "Soon, very soon," he said.

As I climbed down the ladder to the flight deck, the bosun's pipe sounded, followed by the OOD announcing, "Carrier Strike Group 2311, arriving."

Father Rick had the idea that the OOD should follow that announcement with, "*The Keepers of Time*, arriving." Good idea, I told him, but I thought it was best to blow the crews' minds a little bit at a time.

Bill and Magda would meet with the department heads in the wardroom for lunch at 1300. I decided to take them on a tour of the *Reagan* by myself.

We started the tour on the bridge, where I introduced them to Mike Blakely, my XO. Captain Tomlinson was still in sick bay, looking like shit I might add. He would not be part of the tour. I showed Bill and Magda our navigational and communications equipment.

"When we had satellites to rely on, navigation was the simplest thing in the world," I said. "I still find it hard to believe that in the past 210 years only one country, I believe you said China, has the rocket technology to launch a satellite."

"More will come soon," Bill said. "I can't predict when, but the technology is there; it's just a matter of harnessing it. It's also a matter of garnering the political will among warring towns to do something for the common good, not to mention their own damn good. China is no longer the totalitarian state it once was. You can't describe it as a republican democracy yet, but it becomes more liberalized every year. Soon, China will see the wisdom of sharing its satellites with the rest of the world."

I then took them down to the flag bridge, the place where I'd hang out if I still had a strike group to command. Now, as the acting captain, I spend most of my time on the command bridge. We stopped for coffee in CIC, the ship's Combat Information Center. Bill and Magda were no strangers to technology, but I noticed their eyes bugging out as I showed them our capabilities. "Anybody can pick a fight with the *Reagan*," I said, "but winning the fight could prove to be a challenge."

As I observed them interacting, I tried to put my finger on what they reminded me of. It finally dawned on me: They looked like a couple of kids on Christmas morning. What do these people really want from us? I wondered. I think I knew the answer, but I didn't want to wrap my brain around it—just yet.

When we got to the hangar deck, I thought the two of them would faint. They were familiar with modern aircraft—hell, with their archives at *The Bunker*, there was little that they weren't familiar with. They looked at each other, and Bill pointed.

"Oh my God, admiral," he said. "Are we looking at a couple of A-10 *Warthogs?*"

"Yes, you are," I said. "A-10s aren't designed for carriers, but we have these two aboard for special missions. You seldom see an A-10 on a carrier, because the wings don't fold, and it takes a hell of a lot of maneuvering to push these planes around the hangar deck and the flight deck."

"I've read that the A-10 was beginning to fall in disfavor among many military leaders," Bill said. "That always amazed me. The *Warthog* is probably the best plane ever invented for close in ground support."

Good grief, I thought. My gentle intellectual friend Bill seems to know a hell of a lot about military doctrine.

I noticed Magda whisper into Bill's ear. Something was up, but I couldn't figure out what.

After the tour we met in the wardroom with my department heads. I introduced them and, along with Jack and Father Rick, gave them our impressions of what we saw at the Greenbrier, and *The Keepers of Time.*

I handed the video that Bill had made to XO Blakely. "Mike," I said, "please make arrangements for the department heads to view this in groups."

Something didn't feel right. The hours I spent with Bill and Magda gave me the confidence that I could trust them, but I was getting the impression that Bill wanted something from me, something big. I need something from him, too, and I'm not sure he can deliver.

CHAPTER SIXTEEN

A war party of 150 men gathered at the headquarters of Simon McGrath, the warlord of Pittsburgh Town. The meeting's purpose was to plan for the upcoming raid on Philadelphia Town, a distance of over 300 miles.

McGrath had been the leader of Pittsburgh Town for 20 years. He was 59, well past the normal life expectancy of 48 in the towns. He relished the part of his office that included war planning. McGrath insisted that he be referred to as Mayor McGrath, but he was nothing more or less than a warlord, a dictator, a gang leader. He took office after he personally assassinated his predecessor, although he denied it. McGrath loved power in all of its forms. He kept himself surrounded by armed security guards, recalling how he ascended to office.

One of his proudest achievements was the stadium, built five years earlier. He had learned from other warlords how a simple form of entertainment can keep the population calm and satisfied, well at least calm. Warlords never formed friendships, just contacts of convenience. They all found it useful to gather occasionally over the years to exchange ideas. The concept of forming mutually beneficial alliances was an idea that had yet to resurrect itself.

Mayor McGrath had attended gladiatorial events at other town's arenas. He found that the one at what is called the Eastern Empire, especially compelling. To see young people killing one another suited McGrath, especially because the games kept the population occupied. He looked forward to inter-town contests between Pittsburgh and other towns. Although these competitions can occasionally result in crowd violence, it was worth the risk.

The war party would travel to Philadelphia by armored military vehicles. Over the years, most warlords realized that keeping vehicles in working order was a high priority. A specially insulated warehouse enclosed Pittsburgh Town's fleet of 105 assorted vehicles. The best paid jobs in the town went to auto mechanics, the people who kept the ancient vehicles running.

The 150-man war party boarded 25 vehicles, most of which were Humvees, although there were a few old Toyota Land Cruisers in the group. Mounted on top of each vehicle was a machine gun. With six men to a vehicle, the ride shouldn't be too uncomfortable.

The old highways that connected Pittsburgh Town to Philadelphia Town had not been repaired in over 200 years. Although the lack of vehicular traffic over the years somewhat slowed the decay to the road, the journey would be arduous. At a speed limit of 65 miles per hour, a trip in the old days would take about four-and-a-half hours. But the convoy could travel at no more than 30 mph, because of the condition of the road. It would take 10 hours to get to Philadelphia.

Their objective was to steal automotive parts from Philadelphia Town. It was well known that Philadelphia Town had a huge amount of auto parts in a warehouse. Nobody knew why, historically, these parts came into the town's possession. They didn't know because there was no history to read, or if there was, nobody would bother to read it.

McGrath's spies had assured him that Philadelphia Town had no drones or any other kind of aircraft at its disposal. This insured the element of surprise, thought McGrath. Many of his closest lieutenants and advisors were concerned about McGrath's planning abilities. It was widely known among his inner circle that McGrath was simply stupid, and many botched raids and missions attested to that.

The Pittsburgh Town raiding party had just entered what was once known as King of Prussia, Pennsylvania, about 20 miles from Philadelphia Town.

Jonas Blevin, a lieutenant in the Army of Philadelphia Town, looked out over his artillery pieces. He was in charge of a security battery that protected Philadelphia against raids from the west. Under his command were three M198 medium-sized 155 mm howitzers, all aimed at the roadway below the encampment. His five-man battery also had five RPG grenade launchers, 25 rounds of grenades, as well as M16s and small arms of various types.

Sergeant James Rooney walked up to Blevin, laughing.

"Look there, lieutenant. A convoy of 25 armed vehicles. I'll bet that idiot from Pittsburgh Town has ordered another one of his raids."

"Fire on my command," Blevin shouted.

When the Pittsburgh convoy passed in front of them, no more than 100 yards away, Blevin yelled, "Fire!"

Within two minutes all 25 of the Pittsburgh raiding vehicles lay in smoking heaps of rubble. The men who tried to escape were shot under a hail of bullets from M16s.

Another one of Simon McGrath's raids ended up in disaster.

Three weeks later, when Pittsburgh spies confirmed what everyone thought—that the raiding party was attacked and destroyed—Mayor Simon McGrath was assassinated.

Among the many matters that never rose to the top of Mayor McGrath's agenda was a succession plan. There was none. His job—warlord—was popular and sought after. At least 10 people vied for the post, but because the way to get there did not include an election, the campaigning was a matter of deals, violence, and death, with one group of supporters battling other groups. Within a month, Pittsburgh Town was lawless, a place of riots and bloodshed. The yet-to-be completed gladiatorial stadium would never be built. People killed one another in the streets, not the arena.

The electricity failed, then the sewer system backed up. The few medical clinics that existed were abandoned, after crowds raided them to steal drugs. The police force withdrew from the public eye. Law enforcement was in the eyes of the beholder. Pittsburgh Town was doomed, until a new warlord with enough ruthless power took over.

CHAPTER SEVENTEEN

Day Nine

People call me Jack. Some call me Lieutenant Jack, others Lieutenant Thurber. Ashley, the love of my life, calls me honey, my favorite title.

I landed at the Greenbrier for my visit to the journalism section, and I couldn't wait to talk to some of my new journalist friends, the people who keep the present alive by recording the news for the future. Seth Lombardi, the editor-in-chief of *The Daily Keeper,* assembled a staff of 100 reporters in one of the many auditoriums in *The Bunker.*

"Ladies and gentlemen," said Lombardi, "We've read about this man, and some of us have read his books or articles. It isn't often that we get to meet a real live Pulitzer Prize winner. Maybe Jack can tell us how to land the prize, if it ever gets reinstated. Jack, the floor is yours."

"Good morning," I said, "and I thank you for your warm hospitality. I know that Bill Wellfleet has told you about our group and I'm sure that Magda has filled you in as well. As you know, the *USS Ronald Reagan* has come here with over 5,000 people from another time, from 210 years in the past. The morale of our crew is beginning to strain, especially after we saw the devastation of New York City. The Greenbrier has changed that, at least for those of us who have been here. Bill Wellfleet made a video of our last visit and it will be shown to the crew. What began with despair—New York City—has changed into hope. *The Keepers of Time* is a perfect name for your organization. An organization that started back in my time with a wonderful guy named Ezekiel Wellfleet, has matured into the flame of freedom, the flame of the truth. As journalists, you and I have a sacred responsibility to record the truth, the whole truth, as we see it, and to let the chips fall where they may. We all live by a credo that says there can never be enough information, and since the *Big War,* you folks and your ancestors have done just that, you've written and preserved the past. Without the free exchange of information, outposts such as *The Keepers* would not exist. Bill showed us a video that sickened me, a video of a gladiatorial fight between two young women, one of whom I understand was kidnapped from here. We saw a reenactment of a savage time from thousands of years in the past. But we learn that it just happened days ago, here in the present. I can't speak for our leader, my wife, Admiral Ashley Patterson, but I know that she'd agree with me that we'll do everything we can to help your quest during our time with you."

Oh shit. What did I just say? I meant that we'd be cheerleaders and encouragers, especially myself. But did I just float the idea that we'd bring them military assistance? Ashley is gonna be pissed, and I won't blame her. Did I just raise some expectations that I had no right to raise? I better wrap up this speech before I fuck it up any more, I thought.

"Ladies and gentlemen, *The Keepers of Time* stand between the darkness of wanton depravity and the bright sunshine of truth and freedom."

"The crowd went wild" is a hackneyed phrase, but sometimes it's true. Everyone stood and applauded loudly, some cheering, a few standing on their chairs and fist pumping the air. I just hoped that they were cheering my kind words, and not the possibility that I was offering military aid.

After the meeting and a bunch of questions and observations, I sat in an office with Editor-in-Chief Seth Lombardi. It amazed me how the Greenbrier's elegance pervaded even the smallest spaces. No details were left out, including framed clippings of major historical events.

"Jack, you've run organizations a lot bigger than the *The Daily Keeper*. I feel humbled to have you with us. Let me show you something, although I'll understand if you only want to watch part of it. We journalists have to steel ourselves to look at things we'd rather not, so we can turn around and speak the truth. Check this out."

On the monitor in front of him I saw the outline of the stadium I saw the other day. A group of seven people stood huddled together in the middle of the arena. Seth put the video on hold.

"Any guess as to what's about to emerge from those doors, Jack?"

I shook my head.

"Wolves, Jack, a fucking pack of wolves, about to tear those people to shreds. Welcome to *civilization* in the year 2227."

I didn't know what to say. I just stood there. I knew I had an expression on my face that spelled disgust. I was suddenly speechless. Lombardi turned off the video and spun his chair around to face me.

"Jack, you folks are the muscle we need."

⋙ ⋘

While Jack was ashore at the Greenbrier, I went to sick bay to check up on Captain Tomlinson.

"Hey, Harry. How are you feeling?" I said. He looked like death, but I tried to convey a chipper attitude.

"I feel like I'm letting you down, admiral," he said.

"Harry, give me a break. You're not letting anybody down. Your heart just let you down, but that's going to get better. You just rest, relax, and don't worry about anything. I've got you covered."

Harry Tomlinson is a good guy. It hurt me to see him so sick, but sick he was. Looks like I'm going to be the skipper of the *Reagan* for God knows how long.

Father Rick and I met in my office for dinner. I needed to confide in him, and I didn't want to talk in the wardroom. My aide had just set out the dinnerware when Father Rick walked in, his face beaming with his usual smile.

"So what's up, Ashley?"

"I want to talk about morale, Father. I know you've been dining with the crew and keeping your ears open. Talk to me about it."

"Hey Ashley, I dine with the crew every other day because the food's much better than in the wardroom."

He let out a hearty laugh.

"Okay, wiseguy," I said. "What are you hearing from the crew?"

"Ashley, shortly after we hit the wormhole, you gave a typically rousing speech to the crew. You announced that we'd steam along the coast for a month, with one objective, and I'm quoting you, 'The one objective is to find other human beings and communicate with them.' Well, my friend, you may be pleased to know that the crew listens to you when you talk. Here's the bottom line as I heard more times than I can remember. The crew is saying, 'Okay, we found human beings and we communicated with them. It's time to go home.' Those comments were based on your words, Ashley."

Father Rick can be so honest and straightforward it's annoying at times.

"Are you suggesting that we abandon *The Keepers of Time* and just concentrate on finding our way home, Father?"

"I'm not suggesting anything, Ashley. You asked me how the crew is doing and I answered you. They want to go home."

"Well, two things, Father. First, we haven't yet figured out how we'll accomplish our homeward journey. We still have the wormhole problem. I've heard a few ideas, but nothing that convinces me that we have an easy shot at crossing the wormhole in shallow water. The second thing is this, and let me pose it to you as a question: Do we have an obligation to help *The Keepers*, and if so, how?"

"Let me give you a little perspective, my friend," Father Rick said. "You're an admiral, and as such, not just a senior naval officer, but in the strange time we find ourselves, you are the ranking representative of the United States Government. Yes, I know, the United States no longer exists in this year, but the reality is that it's alive and well with the crew of the *USS Ronald Reagan*. And you're the boss."

"You're not being very helpful, Father. I asked you if you think we have an obligation, not just to ourselves, but to that bastion of civilization that we discovered, *The Keepers*. Yes, we're in the future, but the reality is that we are very much here."

"Ashley, remember *The Gray Ship* event?"

"Remember it? How could I possibly forget it? The ship that I commanded slipped through a wormhole and traveled from 2013 to 1861, two days before the Civil War. You were very much there, Father."

"Yes, I was," Father Rick said, "and I want to remind you of the command dilemma you faced. Everybody wanted to hunt for the wormhole and return to the year we came from. But, a certain leader named Ashley Patterson didn't forget her obligation to her country. I recall our countless meetings and arguments. You, Jack, and I agonized over the moral question whether to change history. Well, admiral, you decided that we'd forget about philosophy and do what the situation demanded. After we met with Abraham Lincoln, you concluded that the *USS California* had an obligation to weigh in on the side of the Union and fight the Confederacy. So we did, and we changed history at the Battle of Bull Run. Did we do the wrong thing? Remember, because of your decision, the total casualties in the Civil War turned out to be less than 3,000—not the 600,000 who would have died if you hadn't decided to fight."

"But that was the past, Father. Yes, we changed history, and I'm still convinced that we did so for the better. Help me to understand my current moral position. We know that we're 210 years into the future, a very ugly future. If we change history again, it will be going forward. How can we screw up if I decide to intervene?"

"That's why your pay grade is a lot higher than mine, Ashley. The ultimate decision rests with you."

I was getting the feeling that my friend, Father Rick, was avoiding my question. I know it's my decision, but Father Rick is a man whose opinions I cherish. I decided that I would not let the meeting end without Father Rick coming down on one side or the other.

"At the risk of repeating myself, Father, what do *you* think I should friggin do?"

"I will answer your question, but first let me put things into perspective. We're convinced that *The Keepers of Time* are a bastion, as you called them, of civilization. I want to remind you of something we both saw three days ago. We saw, with our own eyes, a video of two pretty young women fighting to the death for the enjoyment of a crowd soaked in bloodlust. I wish I could banish that from my memory, but I can't, and maybe I shouldn't. I noticed your reaction, Ashley: disgust, tinged with anger. That describes my feelings as well. Now, I'm a man of God, or at least I try to be every day. But turning the other cheek, as Jesus reminded us, does not always mean sitting by and doing nothing. So, in a long-winded answer to your question, Ashley, my answer is *yes*. Yes, we should intervene. To the extent we help to strengthen the forces of civilization and truth, we will be working God's plan."

I smiled and let out a sigh of relief. My good friend, Father Rick, always sees through to the truth, and he just announced it.

Morally we can't let the evil barbaric "towns" attack the outposts of civilization that *The Keepers* occupy. I've got to help.

"Thanks, Father, as usual. You've always helped me to see things with a clear moral telescope, and you just did so."

"So what's the first thing on your mind, admiral?"

"I'm going to blow up that fucking gladiatorial stadium."

CHAPTER EIGHTEEN

"Good morning ladies and gentlemen, Wolf Blitzer reporting for CNN. I wish I could say that we have a positive update on the disturbing disappearance of the *USS Ronald Reagan*, but at this point it remains a mystery. If you've been watching this morning, you know that at 8:45 a.m., the *Reagan*, a huge Nimitz Class nuclear aircraft carrier, suddenly disappeared from sight and from radar screens. The *Reagan* was the flagship of Carrier Strike Group 2311 and was heading toward Boston along with *USS Bunker Hill*, a *Ticonderoga* class missile cruiser, and two frigates, *USS Samuel B. Roberts* and the *USS Stark*. The cruiser and both frigates are all afloat and very much in communication. Whatever happened to the *Reagan* obviously missed those ships. We have with us this morning, retired Admiral Cecil Randolph, a former captain of the *USS Ronald Reagan*."

"Good morning, admiral. Can you help us to understand this bizarre story?"

"In my long Navy career, Wolf, I thought I'd seen everything, but this event has me mystified. The waters off Long Island where the *Reagan* steamed are not extremely deep, maybe 150 feet. How a 101,000-ton ship can suddenly disappear stretches one's imagination. I understand that the other ships have been dropping sonobuoys, which are basically underwater listening devices, but they haven't picked up so much as a ping anywhere near the *Reagan*'s last known position. From what I understand, the *Reagan* sent out no distress signals, or anything that would alert someone that there was a problem. There were no reports of any explosions. The *Reagan* was steaming in plain view of the other ships when it disappeared. Suddenly it was just gone. Also, assuming that the ship sank, the mystery gets worse. A gigantic ship like the *Reagan* would not sink like a stone, no matter how damaged its hull. It would take quite a few minutes for such a large vessel to disappear beneath the surface. But all eyewitnesses thus far report that it was suddenly gone from sight. I wish I could be more helpful, but at this point I'm just as confused as anyone."

"Thank you, admiral. I'm sure we'll be contacting you from time to time for updates."

The *Reagan* had been missing for 30 minutes.

"In other news, ladies and gentlemen, the relationship between the United States and the Islamic Republic of Iran continues to deteriorate. Many hailed the nuclear arms agreement between our two countries, signed in 2015, as an end to Iran's nuclear weapon ambitions. Although hopes remain strong, there have been numerous violations of the inspection protocols between Iran and the United States and its allies. President Reynolds has warned the Iranian government that they run the risk of our re-imposing sanctions if there are any further violations. Particularly troublesome is the Iranian nuclear facility at Natanz, the primary site of Iran's uranium enrichment program. Inspection teams have been repeatedly blocked from entering the site. We will be watching these developments carefully in the days ahead."

CHAPTER NINETEEN

Day 10

Jack and the department heads returned to the *Reagan* at 1500 after their introduction to the wonders of the Greenbrier facility. We met in the wardroom for a lengthy debriefing. I was glad that I sent them ashore. The more input I can get into the workings of the strange and wonderful outfit, *The Keepers,* the better.

The department heads could barely contain themselves, they were so enthusiastic about what they saw. They reported in detail from their notes.

"The one upsetting part of our tour, admiral," said Joe Johnston, the navigator, "was a video that Bill Wellfleet showed us of a gladiatorial stadium in a town called the Eastern Empire. I think I speak for all of us when I say that we almost got physically sick."

"The two pretty young girls, one of whom was kidnapped from The Greenbrier?" I asked.

"Yes. It doesn't appear that civilization has advanced in the past 210 years," Jane Bollard said. "I'm still trying to get those images out of my head, not to mention the enthusiastic roar of the crowd.

It was the most disgusting thing I've ever seen. The only positive thing we can think about are *The Keepers*. They seem to be the only people left of what we understand to be civilization."

It occurred to me that Bill Wellfleet is waging a charm offensive to convince us that they're the good guys, not that I blame him. So far, he's convinced me.

Muriel Parker, the engineering officer, had also sat in on Jack's speech to the journalists. "Wow," said Parker, "Lieutenant Jack speaks as well as he writes. He had those people in the palm of his hands."

The meeting ended at 1745.

⇒+⇐

After the non-stop excitement of the past 10 days, Jack and I decided to have a quiet dinner by ourselves in my office. Jack seemed on edge about something. When Jack's upset, I'm upset. That's the way it is between the two of us.

"Hey, honey, why the sour puss?" I said.

"Ashley, we always shoot straight with one another. That's one of the greatest things about our marriage. There's something I've got to tell you, and I think it's going to make you upset, babe. I'm glad that Muriel Parker liked my speech, because that's what I want to talk to you about. In trying to be friendly I may have put my foot in my mouth—or my head up my ass. I told the crowd, and I quote myself exactly: "We'll do everything we can to help your quest during our time with you."

I reached over and gave Jack's hand a squeeze. I figured I'd let him continue.

"Ashley, I'm afraid I made a promise that I didn't have the authority to make."

"It's not a problem, honey," I said. "You may have paved the way for my next talk with Bill Wellfleet. Let me tell you about my

115

meeting with Father Rick. He's been dining with the crew every couple of days. You know how he loves to do that. He told me that the crew is starting to get cranky, and the reason is because of a promise I made after we came through the wormhole. Remember? I said that our objective was to cruise up and down the coast until we encountered human life, and then we'd communicate. After that, as I promised the crew, we'd concentrate on finding our way home. So you're not the only one to make spontaneous promises, Jack."

"Ashley, you said my statement about helping them may have paved the way for your next meeting with Bill Wellfleet. Mind if I ask what you're planning?"

"Jack, we're American naval officers and we have an obligation to do our duty. I've become convinced that our duty is to provide assistance to *The Keepers*, military assistance if necessary. I want to leave them stronger than when we found them. We owe it to the future of the world."

"Anything specific, babe?" Jack said.

"Yes, I want to make sure that no other young people die fighting in that barbaric stadium."

CHAPTER TWENTY

Robert Jorolomen was the warlord of Hollywood Town. People referred to him as Jo-Jo, but not to his face. Like many warlords in the past two centuries, Jorolomen insisted that people refer to him as "The Mayor."

The original Hollywood was really just a wealthy neighborhood of the larger city of Los Angeles. The current Hollywood Town was larger in area than the original Hollywood.

Like most towns that hadn't been influenced by *The Keepers*, Hollywood Town was a place that didn't know its history. For reasons that nobody understood, the town was populated by many skilled builders, from carpenters and plumbers, to electricians and laborers. In the 200 years since the *Big War*, the town had rebuilt itself, although its appearance looked nothing like the prewar Hollywood.

The mild temperature of the hills provided a perfect atmosphere for building. But, like most areas after the war, the population was small, no more than 75,000, and it included most of what was once Los Angeles.

In the late-21st Century, about 75 years after the *Big War,* a construction crew came across what was once a large building. In the basement they found some well-preserved books recounting the history of a thing called the film industry. The men of the construction crew threw the books into a trash pile. Like so many people after the war, they saw no need to know or understand the past. Their sole reason to live was to make life bearable in the present.

Mayor Jorolomen ordered his assistants to call a meeting of the town leaders. These included construction supervisors, sanitation experts, and his trusted lieutenants who were in charge of keeping the peace—and of keeping him informed about the behavior of the town's citizens.

The meeting was held in Hollywood Stadium, a gladiatorial arena built for the entertainment of the locals. It was a small stadium, with a capacity of no more than 7,000. The meeting would be attended by only 500 people, so there was plenty of room. The most recent gladiatorial fights were two weeks before, and were attended by Jorolomen and his two mistresses. Like most warlords, Jorolomen loved gladiatorial contests, not only for his own enjoyment, but for the diversion it offered the citizens, who may otherwise become restless. The games that day consisted of four hours of combat. 24 men paired off against each other, and the finale consisted of six pairs of women. Jorolomen especially loved the fights between women. One of his mistresses was a former gladiatrix, and had the sword scars on her arms to show for it. He found the scars enticing.

The meeting consisted of reports from leaders of various functions of the town. The subject then turned to the upcoming raid on nearby Pasadena Town, a small organization known for its agriculture.

After the meeting in the stadium, Mayor Jorolomen huddled with his military team of 40 men. The objective, to be carried out in two weeks, was a raid on Pasadena. Their objective would be fresh food, as well as slaves to be sacrificed as gladiators.

"Do you think Jo-Jo knows what he's doing?" one of his lieutenants said to another after the raid meeting ended.

"I have no idea, but who cares? We eat, and we get to watch the fights in the stadium."

Two weeks later, the successful raid yielded 500 pounds of fresh produce and a dozen slaves to be trained to kill and die in the Hollywood Town arena.

CHAPTER TWENTY ONE

Day 11

I quietly asked Father Rick and Jack to meet me in the galley next to my office. I wanted to go over some top level matters with my "kitchen cabinet," Jack and Father Rick. We sat around a small table.

"We've got to get back, and we've got to get back fast," I said. "From what we've heard at the Greenbrier, I'm clear what our mission is. We've got to find our way back to 2017 to warn of the upcoming nuclear war, less than a year away. Our mission has suddenly become a bit more dramatic—to save humanity."

"Ashley," said Father Rick, "you and I have discussed this before. Are you comfortable with changing history?"

"Let me answer your question with a question, Father. Are you comfortable with watching the world end in less than a year, and possibly us with it?"

"I think you've summarized the situation perfectly, Ashley," Father Rick said. "That's why you're an admiral."

"I think we all accept the premise," said Jack, "but the next problem is how to get there. We're back to our problem of the shallow water wormhole. Unless we solve that problem, we may as well resign ourselves to finding a nice place to live out our lives at the Greenbrier."

"Jack, honey," I said, "Your friggin IQ probably matches the combined total on this whole ship. I'm assigning you to be in charge of the task to solve the wormhole problem. I hate to give you a direct order, babe. Do you mind?"

"No, I don't mind being given orders by a pretty admiral, especially one that I sleep with."

Father Rick laughed. "Marrying you two was the most important ceremony I ever performed."

"I've got some ideas," said Jack. "One of the historians with *The Keepers* is also an oceanographer. I'm going to spend a lot of time huddling with him."

⟨⟩

After Father Rick left, Jack and I sat in the galley alone.

"Hey, this is crazy," I said, "let's go to our room."

"*Our* room?" said Jack.

"Let's stop the nonsense, honey," I said. "The crew knows we're married. If we tried to keep our sleeping arrangements secret, they'd think we were nuts. Come on. Let's go to our room and get comfortable."

There was nothing Spartan about my accommodations on the *Reagan*. The Admiral's quarters is nicely appointed and actually decorated to resemble the Red Room in the White House. Former First Lady Nancy Reagan had donated the original furnishings and memorabilia. They included books, photographs of President Reagan, his desk when he was Governor of California, and other pieces of history. It also has a real bedroom and a bathroom (too pretty to call a head) that could be found in any decent home. It was a great place to relax and unwind, and that is exactly what I needed to do.

"Hey Ashley, you look like your wound tighter than a drum. You need to relax and let go of some of that anxiety."

"Jack, honey, I thank God that you're here with me. I hope you don't mind me giving you orders. You're my husband, my lover, and my best friend. I don't know where the word 'subordinate' fits into all that. Any time you disagree with one of my orders, please keep quiet in public. When we're alone you can just tell me to 'shove it.' "

"Well, I'm about to give *you* an order, Ashley. I want you to relax and unwind. I order you take a nice hot shower."

"Will you join me?" I asked.

"What are aides for, admiral? Let me help you out of that uniform."

A *Nimitz* Class aircraft carrier is not exactly a romantic cruise ship. But Jack and I didn't notice. He was right, I needed to relax and unwind, and so did he. After our shower we made love, wonderful, warm, cozy love.

After our love-making, we lay still, our bodies intertwined. I put my face in the crook of Jack's neck.

"Hey," I said. "It's been too long. I keep telling the crew that to maintain readiness we have to drill and drill and drill some more. You and I should think about regular practice exercises, the kind we did tonight. Readiness is essential, don't you agree Jack?"

"I agree, admiral. We need to practice more."

CHAPTER TWENTY TWO

Hamlin Borden was the warlord of what used to be Buffalo, New York, now known as Buffalo Town. He sat in his large, comfortable office overlooking Lake Erie. The waterfront town was well situated for taking in supplies and for loading its few trading products for shipment. He wore his customary clothing, a pair of wool trousers, a long-sleeved knit shirt, covered by a sheepskin fleece to protect against the mid-April cold snap. His hat was leather and wool, the typical kind of hat found in Russia in the early 21st Century. He had no idea how he came into possession of the hat, nor where it was made. Why clutter one's mind thinking about such things, he often wondered.

Hamlin had taken over Buffalo Town 10 years earlier, when he assassinated Jacob Knutsen, his predecessor. At the time, Hamlin was in charge of the town's public safety force, a group of armed thugs. He had no problem with Knutsen's leadership; he just felt that at the age of 29 his time had come. So he killed him, with some help from his subordinates.

Buffalo Town had just experienced a harsher than usual winter, with over a dozen blizzards. Even in mid-April, some small drifts of snow were still visible along the town's unpaved streets. The weather forced a delay in the construction of Hamlin's favorite project, a gladiatorial stadium. He had seen matches as a guest of Simon McGrath, Mayor of Pittsburgh Town. Hamlin thought that Buffalo Town, under the leadership of his predecessor, was neglecting a wonderful source of trading revenue as well as a splendid way to keep the citizens happy. He and McGrath agreed that they would have inter-town games at their prospective stadiums. As the construction continued, Hamlin directed his security force to stage raids on small nearby towns in the former Canada to capture slaves to fight and die in the arena.

Having nothing to do that day, Hamlin took his newest mistress on a sightseeing tour. She was a 17-year-old girl that Hamlin's forces had kidnapped from Rochester Town, some 70 miles to the east. She was tall, at about 5'9," taller than Hamlin's 5'7," had black hair and an athletic body. She would make an excellent gladiatrix once the stadium is built, thought Hamlin, but meanwhile he would enjoy her for himself. Her name was Gloria, a name he had a difficult time remembering because he seldom addressed her by name. The security force had also kidnapped her younger brother, who was put to work in the town's metal fabricating plant. The boy would be an excellent hostage to encourage the girl to fight in the arena when the time came.

Hamlin drove Gloria to see nearby Niagara Falls. He drove his battery-operated SUV, a useful vehicle that was manufactured some 50 years before and kept in excellent operating shape by his skilled mechanics. He had no idea where the car was manufactured or how Buffalo Town came into possession of it, nor did he care. Like most residents of the former America, Hamlin cared only about *now*.

Gloria had never seen Niagara Falls before, and squealed with delight as they approached the beautiful cascading water. From their vantage point they could see a structure that was once known as the Niagara Power Plant, a huge hydroelectric facility that once produced inexpensive electricity. After the *Big War*, it took 50 years before any group saw the usefulness of resurrecting the plant. But the project went nowhere. Warring factions from nearby towns prevented the cooperation that was necessary. So the massive facility remained unused for over 200 years. The only changes were the natural decay and deterioration from years of neglect, as section after section collapsed into the Niagara River.

From there he took Gloria 10 miles south to see the construction site of the stadium. It was made of wood and was about half complete. For some reason, over the years, Buffalo Town had a difficult time training or retaining skilled carpenters. Carpenters tend to be strong young men, and he often sold them as slaves to a town that already had a gladiatorial stadium. It never occurred to Hamlin that such a process tended to dissuade young men to opt for carpentry. One, maybe two years from now, and the construction should be finished, Hamlin told his mistress. She asked him what the stadium was for.

"Games. Wonderful, exciting games," he said. He could picture her, sword in hand, fighting to the death in his proud new stadium.

CHAPTER TWENTY THREE

"Good morning ladies and gentlemen, Shepard Smith here for Fox News. I wish I had some better news for you about the strange disappearance of the *USS Ronald Reagan*. For those of you who just tuned in, the *Reagan* disappeared from sight and from radar earlier this morning while steaming off the coast of Long Island. A massive air and sea rescue operation is now underway, but there has been no trace of the gigantic warship. A special Navy submarine rescue vessel is on its way to the scene, and hopefully it will uncover some clues to this mystery. We have with us Admiral Roland Townsend, Chief of Naval Operations."

"Good morning, Admiral Townsend, and thank you for appearing on Fox News. Can you tell us anything at all about this widening mystery?"

"Shepard, you used the right word. It is indeed a mystery. The *Reagan* was commanded by a fine captain, Harry Tomlinson, an officer with many years of carrier experience. The admiral in command of the strike group is Vice Admiral Ashley Patterson, another fine officer, with whom I've served at sea. We have launched an air and sea rescue operation along with ships from the United States Coast Guard. Beyond that, I have nothing new to report. The search is underway."

"Thank you, admiral, and I'm sure we'll be talking again soon, hopefully to discuss some good news from the rescue operation.

"In other news, ladies and gentlemen, we have heard reports from the State Department that negotiations with Iran over repeated violations of Iran's nuclear deal are grinding slowly. The agreement, which was signed two years ago, calls for Iran to limit its uranium enrichment program, and to allow inspections of its sites. The objective for the United States and its six allied signatories is to prevent Iran from enriching uranium to weapons grade. We will keep you informed as the talks continue."

The *Reagan* had been missing for 45 minutes.

⇒⊣+⊢⇐

Day 12

"Admiral, this is Father Rick. May I have a word with you?"

"Sure. Come on up to my office, Father."

"Good morning, Father. Why don't I see that normal smile on your face?"

"I've got some serious matters to discuss, Ashley, and it's not all happy. As you know I've been dining in the crew's mess and chatting with different sailors at every meal. They're not a happy bunch. As of today, we've been gone for 12 days, and the crew is starting to get antsy. I remind you about your speech shortly after we went through the wormhole. I remind you that you said our mission was to find people, communicate with them and then try to return home."

"Well, Father, our mission is on target. We've met people, we've communicated. Now our job is to get the hell out of here. After the staff sees the video of our meeting at the Greenbrier and Bill Wellfleet's speech about the *Big War*, they'll see that our return mission has some urgency. You and I have discussed this. Jack is going to the Greenbrier today to meet with an oceanographer. Our total attention is on the wormhole problem, the shallow water problem. If anybody can come up with a solution, it's Brainiac Jack. Nobody wants to return to 2017 more than me. For now, just tell the crew that our exploring days are over. We're going home. How, we don't know yet, but we're definitely going home. I'm about to meet with Dennis Ciano, the Chief Master at Arms. I want to pick his brain about evidence, the kind of evidence I'll need to take to the White House to convince them that there's a war to prevent."

Father Rick left my office in a better mood than when he entered. I can always count on him to keep me up to date on the crew's morale. They're getting "antsy," as he said, and I don't blame them. So am I.

The helicopter set down on the lawn in front of the Greenbrier and Jack climbed down the ladder. An assistant met him and escorted him into the main lobby. Waiting for him was Walter Greenstone, one of the *Keepers*. Besides being a historian, Greenstone also trained himself in oceanography. They walked about a quarter of a mile to an area of *The Bunker* where oceanographic records were kept.

"Jack, I understand the problem and I hope I may have a solution," Greenstone said. "When the *Reagan* passed through the wormhole, you found yourselves aground, not hard aground, but definitely sitting on the ocean floor. The reason for that is obvious, as you folks have already figured out. Over the 210 years since the war, the seabed off Long Island has changed. You thought you were in plenty of water, and you were, *before* you hit the wormhole. Let me show you some charts that were kept over the years, showing the gradual change to the seabed. Tell me what you notice as you look from chart to chart."

"Wow," said Jack, "when I look at it graphically one thing jumps out at me. Although the distance from shore increased over the years, one thing remains constant: at one point the seabed slopes downward—sharply."

"It certainly does, Jack. Now from what you folks have told me, when you found yourselves aground, you used your propellers— I believe you called them bow and stern thrusters—to inch the ship sideways until you hit deep water. I believe you said it only took a matter of minutes. That's actually great news. Shorelines behave in predictable patterns. You seldom, if ever, see a large variation of the drop-off point. It's uniform, meaning that the seabed takes a sharp downward slope all at once along the coastline. From the facts you've given me, I think there is a maximum of 75 to 100 yards of sand before the shoreline drops off suddenly. Looking at the old charts, we can see that the drop-off becomes dramatic after just a few yards. It's like a wall of sand, and then a sudden abyss."

"So what's your recommendation, Walter?"

"You have a massive underwater engineering and demolition project in front of you. The way I size it up, what you need to do is place heavy explosive charges under the sand near the drop-off point. You will need to place the charges at uniform distances for a minimum of one mile. When the explosives are detonated, you will create a massive landslide, an avalanche of sand. Then you can take sonar readings to see if you have enough depth to navigate toward the wormhole."

"Another problem, Walter," Jack said. "We have what we believe to be an accurate navigational fix for the location of the wormhole, but how do we keep our eye on the wormhole as we're busy planting explosives?"

"I think I may have a solution, Jack. Come with me."

They walked down a series of corridors to a large room that was packed with electronic equipment. Greenstone opened a cabinet and withdrew an object shaped like a hunting rifle.

"This device was invented about 100 years ago," said Greenstone. "Its purpose is to detect electronic and magnetic disturbances in the atmosphere. It's called an Atmospheric Magnetic Detector, or AMD. The purpose was to detect disturbances in the magnetic field around the earth that may have been changed by the nuclear bombs. It works. Now here's where I put on my scientific speculation hat. I believe that the AMD can detect a change in magnetism caused by a wormhole."

"My God," Jack said. "You have a wormhole detector?"

"Correction, Jack. We *may* have a wormhole detector, but I'm 90 percent sure it will work."

"And if it doesn't work?" Jack asked.

"Then you're back to traditional navigation and piloting, maneuvering your work vessels to keep them away from the wormhole while they're planting the explosives. But every scientific bone in my body tells me that the AMD should do the trick. As you know, Jack, *The Keepers* have studied the phenomenon of time travel and wormholes over the years. Of course we don't have definitive experimental data, but we've read countless indications that tell us that a wormhole causes a change in the earth's magnetism in the area around the site. I recommend that you take this information back to the ship and begin making plans. I believe that you have a detachment of folks referred to as Navy SEALs. My reading tells me that they're experts on underwater demolition. Those people will be a critical part of the operation. I'll be happy to accompany you back to the ship to answer any questions."

"Walter, I'm having a strange feeling. I think I'm feeling optimistic—for the first time in many days."

CHAPTER TWENTY FOUR

Nigel Portland, warlord of the Eastern Empire, stood at the head of the table in his conference room. He wore his best navy blue general's outfit, including a sword in a scabbard on his belt, and wide epaulets indicating his self-appointed rank of five-star general. His boots glistened, spit shined by a new slave from a recent raid. Sitting around the table were his war counsel of the Eastern Empire.

Colonel Reginald Sloan, his chief of staff, sat at the opposite end of the table. Sloan, as well as the other officers around the table, wore uniforms that Nigel Portland designed personally. The uniforms were spotless and crisply ironed, as Portland insisted. A few of the officers thought that the swords were a stupid append-age, but none dared express such an opinion in Portland's earshot.

"Colonel Sloan, please give us the readiness report for our at-tack on the Greenbrier," said Portland.

"We're ready to head out tomorrow, general. We have enough vehicles and trailers to accommodate 5,000 men. The new ar-mored vehicles that we obtained from our raid on the Picatinny

Arsenal are a blessing. The distance is 250 miles over rough terrain, so we expect to attack after a ride of about 12 to 14 hours. Our troops will be heavily armed with automatic assault rifles, rocket-propelled grenades, and small arms. They will be backed up with five howitzers, also obtained from Picatinny."

"Gentlemen," said Portland, "this will be the largest raid we've ever conducted. Our target, the Greenbrier and those strange people who call themselves *The Keepers*, will never know what hit them. They are rich in resources, including a large bunker that houses all sorts of electronic equipment, the use of which we don't know. Something to do with information storage and retrieval, whatever that is. They also have a plant for manufacturing small electronic gear, a well-tended farm, and a cattle ranch. We will look to take as many prisoners as possible to help us understand their electronic instruments. Any prisoners who lack the knowledge we need will be sacrificed in the arena. The Greenbrier is well defended, with a military force of at least 2,500 men. We believe they have a few artillery pieces, including mobile howitzers."

Lieutenant Joshua Billings raised his hand.

"Sir, can I ask how we know so much about *The Keepers'* facility?"

"Over the years we have managed to kidnap many people from the facility. They give us all the information we need, whether by torture or by threatening to put them into the arena to fight. That beautiful young woman who lost her head in the arena a few days ago came from the Greenbrier."

"*The Keepers*," Portland continued, "to the best of our knowledge, do not conduct raids on other towns. My sources tell me that they derive revenues from other groups and even foreign countries sharing in a thing called a database. Why people would pay for information is beyond me. Among the large staff of people who work in the bunker are a number of young women, perfect for the arena. The facility also contains a fuel depot and a refining station.

We have no idea how that works, but we'll find out. Anything else, Colonel Sloan?"

"Sir, we begin our journey at 4 a.m. tomorrow morning. We expect to be at our target's doorstep by no later than 6 p.m. with enough daylight to facilitate the raid."

"Gentlemen," said Portland. "We are about to embark on an attack that will forever change the fortunes of the Eastern Empire. Whatever it is that *The Keepers* keep, it will be ours. To celebrate our victory we will have special fights in the arena, using slaves acquired in recent raids."

CHAPTER TWENTY FIVE

Day 13

I was prepared to show the Greenbrier history video to another group of officers before I showed it to the crew. I needed to hear their opinions before I set something loose that I may regret later. The video was to be shown in a briefing room, which is like a small theater.

"Folks, I'm about to show you the video that Bill Wellfleet made for us. Jack, Father Rick, Jane Bollard, and Chief Ciano were there, but I asked them to be here for a second viewing. After I show it, my intention is to play it for the crew over the ship's TV. But first I want your comments. The video will be somewhat upsetting. It shows the *Keeper* folks discussing the run-up to the nuclear war as well as its aftermath, here in what used to be the United States, as well as around the world. I've drawn one conclusion from the lectures: We've got to get the hell out of here and try to get back to 2017. As you watch the video, I think you'll agree."

I hit the button and the video began, starting with Bill Wellfleet's introduction. Jack manned the computer and would stop the action if anybody had a question. We had just gotten to the part about Iran's secret uranium enrichment facility, when suddenly the squawk box rang out.

"Admiral Patterson, this is Commander Drucker on the bridge. Bill Wellfleet is on the radio and says he needs to speak to you urgently."

I stepped out into a passageway to take Wellfleet's call.

"Admiral, Bill Wellfleet here. We're about to be attacked. One of our drones picked up a column of vehicles and mobile howitzers heading straight for the Greenbrier. All of the trucks have machine guns mounted on their roofs. The lead vehicle is carrying the flag of the Eastern Empire."

"Bill, give me some numbers."

"There are at least 100 vehicles plus a few trailers, most of them personnel carriers. They can accommodate up to 5,000 troops. One of our spies warned us that Portland was up to something, but we didn't expect a full assault. With 5,000 soldiers plus artillery, they have the capability to cripple the Greenbrier."

Sometimes command decisions can be agonizing affairs. When you're at the helm and the final decision is yours, it's easy to get caught up in a game of second guessing. What if I do this, but that happens? But sometimes a decision is easy. I just heard that *The Keepers*, an outpost of civilization in a barbaric world, is about to be attacked. They're our friends and allies. This decision was easy. I'm going to destroy their attackers.

"How far out are they, Bill?"

"About three hours from the Greenbrier at the speed they're traveling, admiral."

"How many miles do you estimate the column to be?" I asked.

"Seventy-five, maybe a hundred miles," Wellfleet said.

"Great. I can have my planes over their targets in less than an hour. I'm going to battle stations and we'll commence launching aircraft in 15 minutes. I'm signing off for now. Call me immediately if anything changes. I'll let you know when my planes are on target. Give me the current coordinates of the lead vehicle so I can relay it to my air boss."

"Commander, sound general quarters," I said to the officer of the deck.

The loud clanging of the alarm sounded throughout the ship, followed by, "General quarters, general quarters, all hands man your battle stations. This is not a drill. I repeat, this is not a drill."

I called Phil Lysle, the air wing commander.

"Commander prepare to launch an attack now. I want eight F/A-18s. Coordinates of the target are on their way. The target is a convoy of 100 vehicles on their way to the Greenbrier. I want all of the vehicles destroyed. I'm coming to the bridge now."

I ducked back into the briefing room to let everybody know what was going on. As I walked up to the bridge I gave myself a mental pat on the back. I'm fanatical about operational readiness, and I drill my crew drill constantly to make it happen. That's why we're ready to launch aircraft a few minutes after my command.

I watched the first Super Hornet launch off the flight deck. In 45 minutes, the column of vehicles was visible, and I could see what the lead pilot saw on my video monitor. The planes flew slowly toward their targets. The lead pilot locked onto his target and fired two rockets at the lead truck, which exploded into small pieces. The pilots are well-trained for an assault on a column of vehicles. Each successive plane fired at the next few targets in the convoy. A few vehicles attempted to pull off the road and seek cover in the woods, but they were cut down by rockets. Within less than a minute every vehicle had been hit. The attack convoy was now a smoking pile of rubble. After the eighth plane launched its rockets, the lead pilot turned around to give us a look at the result. Every single target, including the mobile howitzers, was destroyed. Most were no longer recognizable as vehicles. I called Bill Wellfleet on the radio.

"Are you watching this from your drone, Bill?"

"Yes, I am. God bless you, admiral. You've just saved *The Keepers of Time.*"

"I'm not done yet, Bill. I'm going to steam south to get closer to the Arlington area."

"What for, admiral, if you don't mind me asking?"

"I'm going to destroy the Army of the Eastern Empire, starting with that fucking stadium."

I can't believe that I used such profanity over the radio. I really have to watch my mouth. Oh fuck it, I thought, I'm about to strike a blow for civilization.

On the hard drive that Bill Wellfleet had given us were detailed maps of the Eastern Empire, including every building. The map appeared on a computer in the Combat Information Center (CIC). I called Phil Lysle, the air boss, and Major Clark of the Marine detachment. We poured over the maps, picking targets. *The Keepers* people, no surprise, had carefully labeled every structure on the maps, including a weapons depot, the command center (Portland's house), the army barracks, and a power plant. Also labeled were housing facilities, which I wanted to avoid. What didn't need labeling, but it was labeled anyway, was the gladiatorial stadium. The stadium was made of wood, so I told Phil Lysle that I wanted it attacked with incendiary bombs and rockets.

"Our objective, gentlemen, is to degrade or possibly destroy their ability to make war. I want to avoid hitting innocents. According to Bill Wellfleet, the Eastern Empire keeps a large number of slaves, including people abducted from *The Keepers.* Avoid striking any of the buildings that are marked as housing."

We would reach our launch area in an hour.

CHAPTER TWENTY SIX

"General Portland, may I see you sir?" said Lieutenant Joshua Billings, Portland's aide.

"What is it lieutenant? The convoy isn't due to arrive at Greenbrier for three hours."

"Something may have happened to the war party, sir. The last message we received was a couple of minutes ago. All we heard were shouts and explosions. I fear that the convoy may have been intercepted. The only intelligible word we could hear was 'planes.' "

"How can this be possible?" said Portland.

"Well, sir, as you know, we've received reports of a gigantic ancient aircraft carrier plying the waters off the coast. Our spies have told us that the command of the ship has been in contact with the Greenbrier. We also know that *The Keepers* use drone surveillance aircraft. It's possible that our convoy was spotted and then intercepted by planes from the aircraft carrier."

"Any response to radio calls?"

"No, sir. Absolute silence. I fear that our war party has been destroyed."

"What's that sound?" said Portland.

The two men stepped out onto the deck and looked up. In the final moment of their lives, they saw an F/A-18 release a 500-pound bomb at the building.

Three jets targeted the site that was marked as the weapons depot. The building was almost stacked to capacity with weapons and ordnance from the raid on the Picatinny Arsenal. The explosion was so large and intense, a mushroom cloud formed over the building. Secondary explosions from bombs, rockets, grenades, and small-caliber ammunition continued for an hour.

Four of the super Hornets streaked toward the wooden gladiatorial stadium. Wellfleet had assured me, from his spies, that no games were scheduled for that day. The jets fired incendiary rockets at four lower quadrants of the structure. Within minutes, the stadium that brought glee to the hearts of bloodthirsty spectators, was totally engulfed in flames. After five minutes, the structure collapsed in on itself.

Jack and Father Rick were standing next to me in CIC, watching the bombing results on video monitors. When the stadium went up in flames, I turned to Father Rick and said, "My prayers have been answered."

The Army of the Eastern Empire, and possibly the Empire itself, was in ruins.

I called Bill Wellfleet on the radio.

"Bill, I don't know if all your problems are over, but any problems you expected from Portland and his gang are done with. The Eastern Empire no longer exists. I'm sending in helicopters and the Marine detachment to look for survivors."

"Please tend to their needs, admiral. We have plenty of room at the Greenbrier for refugees. Many of them will be our former neighbors, no doubt. Again, God bless you."

CHAPTER TWENTY SEVEN

"Good morning ladies and gentlemen, Chris Wallace reporting for Fox News Sunday. We have a special segment to show you this morning from the Oval Office, where I'll interview President Reynolds about the deepening crisis with Iran over its violations of the nuclear agreement. The interview will be broadcast in its entirety right after this message from our sponsors."

"Chris, I'm not going to bullshit you, my friend," said President Reynolds as the microphone was being attached to his lapel. "We're dealing with a hot potato here, and it's only going to get hotter. Don't be afraid to dig deep for answers, because that's what the American people deserve."

The producer counted down to air time, and the interview began.

"Hello again, ladies and gentlemen, Chris Wallace in the Oval Office for Fox News Sunday. I'm here with President Reynolds, and our main topic of conversation will be the problems with the Iranian government and the repeated violations of the nuclear agreement of 2015.

"Mr. President, a story that has moved to the front pages recently concerns the violations of the nuclear accord with Iran. I know that you have serious concerns, sir, about the stability of the current negotiations."

"Chris, as you know, I opposed to the nuclear agreement from the start. I made my opposition quite clear during my election campaign. We're now getting a barrage of intelligence data that Iran is not only in technical violation, but that it may be enriching weapons-grade uranium at facilities other than Natanz, facilities that were not disclosed during the talks. Yes, you heard me correctly, we have information that Iran is involved in uranium enrichment far beyond the terms of the agreement, and that the sites of the enrichment program were never disclosed. The agreement was passed by Congress with all sorts of trigger points for possible violations, and those trigger points have been far exceeded. I don't want to sound overly political, but it appears that there are a lot of senators and congressmen who are covering their backs for supporting a bad deal. Congress is adamant that we should be patient, and that everything will be okay. Did you ever hear the phrase, 'Peace in our time'? Yes, it's the infamous statement of Neville Chamberlain at Munich, Germany, in 1938, arguing for patience with Adolf Hitler. We know how that worked out. Chris, the American people are being stonewalled, and our own Congress is providing the stones."

"Mr. President, are there any other security matters that have you concerned?"

"Yes, there certainly are. Our satellite surveillance has shown a large increase in shipping activity between Iran and North Korea, activity that cannot be explained by normal analysis of commercial actions. Combine that activity with the increasing number of violations of our agreement, and we're looking at concerted action that goes the very heart of the suppose deal. I'm very concerned about the national security implications for the United States and our Western allies, and I think your viewers should be concerned too."

"Thank you Mr. President. You have certainly given our audience some electrifying news to digest."

The camera cut to Chris Wallace, indicating that the interview was at an end.

"Thank you for watching, ladies and gentlemen. We will be tracking these unfolding events in the days and weeks ahead."

"Chris," said President Reynolds as the crew was removing his microphone, "keep on top of this story. It's not going away."

A large freighter bearing the flag of Norway took on a shipment at the Iranian southern port city of Bandar Abbas. The cargo consisted of 80 wooden boxes, measuring 4' by 3' by 6.' The city was strategically located on the Strait of Hormuz. Bandar Abbas is also the main base of the Iranian Navy. After loading was complete, the freighter began its journey, not to Norway, but to North Korea.

CHAPTER TWENTY EIGHT

Day 14

I maneuvered the *Sea King* off the flight deck of the *Reagan* into a gentle breeze. This would be my final flight of what we had begun to call the *Greenbrier Shuttle.* Jack and Father Rick were with me. Our goodbye to the Wellfleets and the other people at the Greenbrier was likely to be emotional. Under the weird circumstances we found ourselves in, relationships tend to intensify. We all thought of *The Keepers* as friends, good friends.

I set the helo down on the lawn in front of the main building, thinking about how I was going to miss the beautiful view of the elegant old place.

Magda greeted us in the main lobby. She wore a smartly tailored black sheath with a bright pink cummerbund that looked like it came out of Saks Fifth Avenue.

"Dahlings, I'm enchanted as usual," said Magda in her theatrical way. For Magda, the world is her stage. "Come, join me," she said.

She led us into Bill Wellfleet's office. He stood and quickly walked over to us to shake our hands.

"I've said it before, but that was over the radio," Bill Wellfleet said. "I now get to thank you in person. You've saved *The Keepers* from a threat that could have destroyed us. The Eastern Empire no longer is a force, thanks to you and the firepower from the *Reagan*. God bless you, Admiral Ashley. *The Keepers of Time* live on, because you."

Bill looked like he was about to break down in tears.

"Attacking that war party and destroying the Eastern Empire were among the easiest command decisions I ever had to make, Bill, but we all appreciate your gratitude. When I heard our friends were about to be attacked, I knew what I had to do. To change the subject, you know why we're here today. It's time for us to return to where we came from. Our obligation is to warn our government about what will happen on April 12, 2018."

"Admiral, I have a suggestion that might shock you. Magda and I would like to accompany you back to 2017."

"What?" I said, "You're the leader of this wonderful group of people. I know the historian in you is fascinated by the idea of time travel, but are you sure it's a good idea for *you* and *The Keepers?*"

"Magda and I have discussed this thoroughly. *The Keepers* will be in good hands with successor leadership, my nephew Joshua Wellfleet. No, I'm not suggesting this as a curious historian. I think that we may prove to be a vital part of your plans. I suggest that you take a backup of part of our database. You'll need the evidence about the run-up to the *Big War* to convince your government that a threat is imminent. I don't expect that you would approach your president and say, 'Hey, we met a nice group of folks from 210 years into the future who convinced us that the country is in danger.' No, you're going to need hard evidence, and you'll need me there to help retrieve it from the database and to interpret the information."

"If we accomplish our mission," said Father Rick, "what if you want to return to the present time?"

"From everything you folks have taught me about wormholes, Father, I think it would be a simple matter of taking a boat through the wormhole, and heading south."

"I'm leaving behind a gift, my friend," I said. "I'm giving you one of our shore excursion boats to follow us to Long Island. I think it's important that *The Keepers* have a record of us going through the wormhole. After photographing us going through the wormhole, they can keep the boat in Baltimore. I'm also giving them a helicopter drone and extra ammunition. I'm sure my government won't mind that I helped out an ally."

"God bless you, Ashley," Bill said.

"Okay, you've convinced me, Bill," I said. "You and Magda are welcome to be my guests for the ride of your lives."

<hr />

I set the helicopter down on the *Reagan*'s flight deck. Our new guests, Bill and Magda Wellfleet, were with us. Once I agreed to take them aboard, I was surprised to find that they had already packed their bags. I guessed that Bill was sure he could convince me. He did. His argument that he could help us present the evidence to the government nailed it for me.

I ordered the navigator to set a course for Eastern Long Island, the place where the wormhole lurked. Last night was clear with millions of stars visible. The navigator took a series of celestial fixes. They confirmed that our internal navigation system was working perfectly. Locating the wormhole will be easy. The hard part will come after that—getting enough water under the *Reagan* to enable us to pass through time.

My phone rang. The phone in my office was only to be used for emergencies. "Admiral Patterson here."

"Admiral, it's George Molloy, the medical officer. I'm afraid I have some bad news, ma'am. Captain Tomlinson has passed away. Shall I contact Father Rick to arrange for burial at sea?"

"No, commander, don't do that. You may think I'm crazy, but I want you to put him in deep freeze. I want to follow my instincts and see if a trip through time will make a difference. I've been through this before. Just humor me, commander. Once we pass through the wormhole I'll make my final decision. Get him in deep freeze now."

CHAPTER TWENTY NINE

"Martha MacCallum for Fox News, ladies and gentlemen, with an update on the strange disappearance of the *USS Ronald Reagan*. As anybody who's watched the news earlier knows, the gigantic warship went missing this morning, and there is no trace of where it is or what happened. At 8:45 a.m. the *Reagan* suddenly disappeared. It's now 10:30, and the ship has been gone for almost two hours. Of course, a massive sea and air rescue operation is under way at this moment. We have with us by live feed, Lieutenant Commander Andrew Pierce of the United States Coast Guard. He commands the Coast Guard cutter, *USCG Harriet*, one of the ships that's looking for the *Reagan*."

"Good morning, commander, can you give us an update on the search and rescue operation?"

"All I can say is that we're still looking. We're looking for any sign at all that might show us what happened. Nothing. No sonar pings, no visual sightings, nothing. *The Reagan* is simply not in view, and we have no idea where she is."

"Thank you commander, and we wish you Godspeed in your search."

"Ladies and gentlemen, the most mysterious story we've covered in a long time is still a mystery. We'll break into our regular broadcast to bring you any new information on the strange disappearance of this Navy ship.

The *Reagan* had been missing for 90 minutes.

Day 15

As we steamed toward Long Island, I spent almost all of my time in my office, meeting with the people who would put Jack and Greenstone's plan into practice—blasting away enough sand to create an underwater landslide and give the *Reagan* sea room to perform our most vital task, steaming through the wormhole. The final plan was simple, and scary. If it didn't work, we'd have a problem.

I became convinced, as did everybody, that to blast away the sand shelf off Long Island, we would use bunker busters, the most fearsome bombs this side of nuclear. The *Reagan* carried a supply of 30 GBU-28s. Each of them was 18.5 feet long and 15.3 inches in diameter, and weighed 5,000 pounds. The bombs were designed to penetrate hardened underground Iraqi command bunkers in the First Gulf War.

We first worked on the idea that the bombs would be placed into the sand by Navy SEALs. A consensus finally developed, because of Jack's urging, that the bombs should be delivered by aircraft to maximize their penetration. We were all convinced that if these bombs could stab deep into the ground and destroy a bunker, penetrating sand should not be a problem. The plan was to drop 10 of the bombs along the sand shelf. Our F/A 118s had been modified to enable them to carry the weapons. The planes, evenly spaced at a distance of an eighth of a mile, would all release their payloads at the same time, maximizing the explosive force.

At 1015 the coast of Long Island became visible. Jack stood next to me on the bridge, along with Bill and Magda Wellfleet. Although it was cool at 60 degrees, my armpits felt like I was in a sauna. Nervous didn't describe the way I felt. Jack leaned over to me and whispered in my ear, "Relax, baby, you're doing great. This is going to work." Have I mentioned that Jack is my best friend?

We arrived at the launch coordinate, and I ordered the jets to take off. As each plane shot off the flight deck, the crew let out a loud cheer. I hoped we'd still be cheering in a few minutes.

We steamed slowly five miles off shore as the planes took their positions. Jack and I stood on the weather deck on the starboard side of the bridge and watched as the planes dove toward their watery targets. We saw the bombs release, and held our breaths. Within a few seconds, we heard a series of muffled explosions. Pillars of water shot up over the blast sites. A huge wave came our way. "That's just what we hoped would happen," Jack said. "It indicates an underwater landslide."

I pointed the bow of the *Reagan* toward the wave to absorb its impact. Then I swung the ship into the wind to retrieve the aircraft.

Then there was silence, a sickening silence. Did it work? It would take a while to find out, because the water was clouded after the explosions. When the sea calmed down I launched four helicopters to drop sonobuoys to determine the depth in a straight line along the coast, with the wormhole in the middle of the line. Each pilot reported the water depth in predetermined order.

"Three hundred feet," shouted the first pilot. "Three hundred" said the second. The third and fourth both said the same beautiful number, 300 feet. They continued along the coast to determine how wide our operating area would be. The plan had worked perfectly. Our bunker busters caused a gigantic underwater landslide, sending the coastline to the ocean floor along a 10-mile line, more than enough room for the *Reagan* to maneuver.

The shrill whistle of the bosun's pipe sounded throughout the ship.

"Attention all hands, attention all hands, attention to Admiral Ashley Patterson."

"Good morning, everyone," I said into the microphone on the bridge. "The explosions you heard a few minutes ago were the sounds of success. We've managed to blast away enough coastline to give the *Reagan* room to maneuver to the wormhole, our doorway to home. We're about to begin the operation right now. Be prepared for a shocking experience. That is all."

The roar of a few thousand sailors rang in my ears. I hoped their cheers weren't premature. Now comes the main act. I popped a Maalox.

"Steer directly toward the coordinates of the wormhole, commander," I said to the navigator.

We steamed at 20 knots, the same speed as when we hit the wormhole 15 days before. Jack squeezed my hand. He's always there for me. He gives me strength. That said, I was still scared out of my mind. To calm myself, I turned to Bill and Magda Wellfleet and said. "You're about to time travel, folks. I hope you enjoy the trip."

A sailor on the bow aimed the Atmospheric Magnetic Detector, or AMD at the place where the wormhole should be. He reported over the radio, "large spike in electromagnetic activity." Walter Greenstone's "wormhole detector" seemed to be working. I ordered a small drone launched toward the coordinates. It disappeared, as we hoped, presumably into the wormhole. So far, so good.

The motor launch that I gave to *The Keepers* was 50 yards off our port beam. The Greenbrier journalists on board were snapping photos.

"One thousand yards to the coordinate, admiral, said the navigator, "five hundred yards, 200, 100..."

The bright late morning sunlight suddenly turned pitch black as the *Reagan* shuddered. Jack turned the backlight on his watch and counted, "One minute, half a minute, 15 seconds, YESSS," he yelled as the darkness returned to daylight. We all looked to starboard. Before our eyes, in their sunlit glory, were the beautiful mansions of the Hamptons. I also noticed, as did the suddenly nervous officer of the deck, that we were surrounded by vessels of all types, including Coast Guard cutters.

I looked at the clock on the bulkhead. It was 1045, exactly two hours after we slipped through the wormhole into the future. My God, I thought, we'd only been gone for two hours. I retraced the past two weeks in my mind, and just shook my head. Time travel is weird. No other way to describe it.

Petty officer nurse Melissa Demming sat at her desk in sick bay, filling out reports on the past two day's sick calls. She wanted to join the cheering up on deck, but she had orders to finish the reports. She heard a pounding on the door of the medical department freezer, and ran over to open it.

"What the hell am I doing in here?" said Captain Tomlinson, standing in his hospital robe. "Get me a blanket."

"Do you feel okay, sir?" said Demming, her eyes as wide as saucers.

"Except for freezing my ass off, I feel fine. Get me Admiral Patterson on the phone."

"Admiral, it's Captain Tomlinson on the line for you," said the OOD.

I grabbed the phone, trying to avoid breaking down in tears.

"Harry," I screamed. "We thought we lost you. How are you feeling?"

"I feel fine except some bozo put me in the freezer."

"Harry, we just went back through the wormhole. I want you checked out by the medical officer. Then you can come up to the bridge and enjoy the show."

The ship thundered with screams and shouts. The vessels around us all blew their horns. We were home. I ducked my head into the bridge. "Give me an intro, commander," as I picked up the microphone. Father Rick had just entered the bridge, beaming his usual bright smile. I leaned over and said, "After I speak, Father, let's have a prayer for the crew."

After the bosun's pipe silenced, I said, "We're home! God bless America, God bless the *USS Ronald Reagan*, and God bless all of you. Attention to Father Rick, who will lead us in prayer."

"Heavenly Father," said Father Rick, "please bless those of us in peril on the sea, and thank you for returning us home safely from our journey. In your Holy Name, we pray. Amen."

"Admiral Patterson, it's Admiral Townsend on the line, ma'am," said the OOD.

Admiral Roland Townsend is the Chief of Naval Operations and a good friend. We served together on the *USS Theodore Roosevelt*.

"Ashley, it's Rolly Townsend here. At the risk of asking an obvious question, where the hell have you been?"

"To get right to the point, admiral (I never called him Rolly in public), for 15 days we've been in the year 2227, 210 years into the future."

"My God, Ashley, did you pull another *Gray Ship* stunt?"

"I'm looking forward to telling you all about it, admiral, and I don't doubt that you're going to call a Naval Board of Inquiry."

"Well, yes, Ashley. I have no choice but to appoint a Board of Inquiry. But for now your orders have been changed. Under the circumstances I can't have your strike group heading toward the Gulf until we find out what happened. Set your course for Norfolk and return to your homeport. I've already alerted the White House."

"Ma'am, it's the President of the United States on line two," said the OOD.

"Rolly, I've got to hang up. The President is calling."

I took a deep breath and hit line two.

"Good morning, Mr. President, Admiral Patterson here. I guess I've got some explaining to do."

'"Admiral Patterson, I speak for the entire country when I say that it's great to have you back, not that I have any idea where the hell you've been. I want to see you in the White House tomorrow. You can take off from the carrier and fly to D. C. Bring any other people you deem appropriate. We're going to take some photos, of course, but then I want you to explain to me what happened."

"Yes, sir, Mr. President."

CHAPTER THIRTY

B ill Wellfleet's introduction to 2017 would happen sooner than he expected. I wanted him with me when I met President Reynolds. My job, my only job, was to convince the president that the nuclear shit will hit the fan in less than a year. Bill Wellfleet was the way to do that.

Bill was dressed in his usual preppy best, but I convinced him to wear a tie to meet President Reynolds.

We launched off the deck of the *Reagan* in a COD (Carrier Onboard Delivery), which is basically a flying delivery truck for assorted stuff including mail. It was roomy enough to hold Bill and Magda, as well as Jack and me. We landed at Joint Base Andrews in Maryland. In 2009 Andrews Air Force Base merged with Naval Air Facility, Washington, to form the new Joint Base Andrews. A limousine drove us to the White House, about 20 miles away. Bill didn't appear in the least bit nervous. He and Magda chatted non-stop about the sights they took in. I was nervous enough for all of us. I had been to the White House before, once on a school trip as a kid, and once for a special reception when I made vice admiral.

No matter how many times you visit the place, it always has a certain majesty to it.

Bill and I had discussed at length exactly what our approach to the President would be. I suggested that we adopt a simple strategy. We would just tell the truth, the exact truth about what happened to the *Reagan*, and how I came to meet Bill, 210 years into the future. Time travel is no longer a phenomenon limited to science fiction novels, and President Reynolds knows that, although he has a reputation as a skeptical man.

We were greeted at the door by a Marine guard and escorted inside.

"Everything is exactly what I expected from the old photographs," Bill said to me.

The Marine guard led us to the Oval Office. President Reynolds stood behind his desk and smiled.

"Admiral Patterson, so good to see you again."

"Mr. President, let me introduce Bill Wellfleet, a man we met on our recent trip."

Reynolds walked from around his desk and shook Bill's hand. He led us to a seating area, more conducive to talking than having the President ensconced behind his desk.

"So, Admiral Patterson, you are the commander of Carrier Strike Group 2311, and suddenly the *USS Ronald Reagan*, your flagship, disappeared for two hours yesterday. It's time to tell your Commander in Chief exactly what happened."

"Sir, to the extent that you know me, you know that I have a reputation as a straight shooter, so that's exactly what I'm going to do. Bill Wellfleet and I are going to tell you the truth, the simple unvarnished truth. At 8:45 a.m. yesterday morning, the *Reagan* traveled in time after slipping through a wormhole, or time portal, off the shore of Eastern Long Island. We went from the year 2017 to the year 2227, 210 years into the future. We traveled along the coast to New York City and discovered that it had been destroyed by nuclear bombs. A metallurgist aboard ship estimated that the event occurred over 200 years in the past. Then we traveled south and came upon a couple of people who took us to see Bill here. He was located in White Sulphur Springs, West Virginia, at the Greenbrier resort. You may recall that the resort includes a gigantic bunker built into a hill that was intended to serve as the seat of government in the event of a nuclear war. That plan was abandoned, as you know, in the 1990s. Bill Wellfleet is the man in charge of a group of people known as *The Keepers of Time*. His distant grandfather, Ezekiel Wellfleet, is the man who began the organization at the Greenbrier. The critical message we're here to deliver to you, sir, is this: On April 12, 2018, less than a year from now, the United States will be attacked by nuclear weapons from Iran and North Korea. April 12, 2018 will be the end of history as we know it. In the year we visited, the United States no longer exists. It had been destroyed in the nuclear attacks, and the only vestiges of civilization in North America is this group called *The Keepers of Time*."

Reynolds stood and walked over to the window. He put his hands on his hips and looked out over the lawn. He walked back to us and sat with his hands on his knees, staring at us and not saying a word. Reynolds has a reputation for controlling conversations, and he sure as hell was controlling this one.

"Admiral Patterson," Reynolds said, "I have not only met you before, but I'm quite familiar with your stories of time travel. I studied the findings of the Naval Board of Inquiry after the bizarre *Gray Ship* incident a few years ago. The board unanimously found that you and the crewmembers of the *USS California* had traveled through time to the Civil War. I repeat, a group of hard-nosed admirals found *unanimously* that you were telling the truth. I also recall seeing photos of you and Abraham Lincoln that a photographic expert swore were true and accurate. Now you're sitting here in front of me and telling me about another incident of time travel. I have to admit that you have a lot of credibility around here. But I want you to put yourself in my shoes. I'm quite serious. A lot of talk around here is that Ashley Patterson may someday occupy this office. So as a person with credibility in this government, and with me in particular, what should I do? More specifically, besides your statements, do you have any objective intelligence you can give me? You're asking me to go to war. I need a lot of actionable data to convince our allies."

"Mr. President, I'm going to ask Bill Wellfleet to respond to that."

Reynolds looked at Bill.

"How old are you, Mr. Wellfleet?"

"Forty-three years old, sir."

"So forty-three plus 210 makes you 253 years old. Before you leave here I want a copy of your diet and exercise program."

We laughed. Reynolds' reputation includes a talent for lightening up tense conversations.

"Mr. President, as Admiral Patterson said, I am the leader of a group of people called *The Keepers of Time*. I have with me, which I shall give to you, a backup of the portion of our database from the two years leading up to the nuclear war and the years after it. The information from the years after the war is especially important. Some survivors from the leadership in both Iran and North Korea were interviewed by a reporter from the *New York Times*—yes, the *Times* still existed for a few years after the war, although most of its staff had been killed. According to a former government official from Iran, they had not only violated the nuclear agreement of 2015, but they secretly constructed a huge underground bunker not far from Natanz, their main plant for enriching uranium. It exists right now, as we speak, and I'm afraid that your intelligence agencies are unaware of it. Not only have they accelerated their uranium enrichment program, they are doing so at bomb-grade level. Iran has also entered into a secret agreement with North Korea, and is shipping nuclear weapons to that rogue state right now. Both Iran and North Korea will attack American cities with nuclear warheads using short-range ballistic missiles. I'm aware of the amusing newspaper reports of North Korea constantly launching ICBMs only to see them splash in the ocean. Those activities are nothing more than an elaborate ruse to convince you that North Korea was seeking to perfect an intercontinental ballistic missile. Nothing could be farther from the truth. They will attack you from commercial ships using short- range missiles."

"Mr. Wellfleet," said the President, "I shouldn't tell you this because you don't have security clearance—hell, you're not even an American citizen—but we're involved in very sensitive negotiations with Iran right now."

"Allow me to show you—not tell you, show you—where those negotiations are headed." Bill said. "Admiral, please show the President the newspaper you obtained from Atlantic City."

Bill had an excellent sense of drama, and I loved how he introduced what I was about to show the President.

"Mr. President," I said. "In our exploration along the coast, I sent a scouting unit ashore at Atlantic City, New Jersey. From the sea, it was obvious that it didn't sustain a direct hit in the attacks. Here is a newspaper that my men found in a newsstand locker in a casino. It was meant for distribution the next day. You can see that it's dated April 12, 2018, less than a year from now, the day that the world will end."

I handed Reynolds the paper.

Nuclear Talks between Iran and the United States Falter
Reports of large amounts of Iranian weapons delivered North Korea
President Puts Military on High Alert

The President read the article, then looked at me without saying anything.

He then turned to Bill Wellfleet and said softly, "Was my family and I here when it happened?"

"Yes, Mr. President. You, your family, and 90 percent of the government were killed, or I should say, will be killed."

Reynolds then looked at me.

"Mr. President," I said, "It's time to sound general quarters and man our battle stations."

CHAPTER THIRTY ONE

"Good morning, this is Roberta Simmons with *The New York Times*. May I please speak to Mr. Ezekiel Wellfleet?"

Roberta Simmons was 35 years old. She stood at 5'9," had long blond hair, and a shapely athletic figure. She lost her husband to cancer five years before, and hadn't remarried. She had no children.

Ezekiel Wellfleet, or Zeke, loved to talk to reporters. He considered it an important part of his mission. He picked up the phone.

"Zeke Wellfleet here. Good morning, Ms. Simmons. What can I do for you?"

"Sir, I'm working on a feature article for the *New York Times* about your plans for the Greenbrier Resort, and I'd love come there and interview you."

"Well, you can call me 'sir,' if you wish, but I answer to Zeke. I'd love to have you drop by. I'll make sure we give you a special room. Okay if I call you Roberta?"

"Please call me Bobbi, Zeke. Will tomorrow be okay?"

"I look forward to seeing you, Bobbi. I love free publicity."

Bobbi Simmons was on assignment in Charlotte, North Carolina, so the trip to White Sulphur Springs, West Virginia, took just under four hours. She left early and arrived at the Greenbrier at 10 a.m.

A uniformed bellman greeted her warmly and took her bag. Her room, as Zeke Wellfleet had promised, was beautiful, with a view of the surrounding hills. Maybe I can stretch this assignment out a few days, she thought. The bellman led her into the main lobby, where Zeke Wellfleet awaited her.

Zeke Wellfleet, age 42, was 5'10." He had medium length sandy brown hair, which complemented his brown eyes. Bobbi looked at his suit. That probably cost more than my five- year clothing budget, she thought. Zeke, she noticed, had a nervous energy about him, not rare for entrepreneurs that she'd interviewed. She also noticed that he was quite good looking. Zeke led her into the main dining room where a table in the corner awaited them.

Zeke flashed a smile that never seemed to go away.

"So, Bobbi, you're here to interview a man who everybody seems to think is a nut."

"Well I wouldn't describe you as a nut, but you do have a reputation for being somewhat eccentric. Can you tell me about this grand experiment of yours? People have said that you're a survival enthusiast, a prepper, a doomsday prophet. But first, tell me a bit about yourself."

"As you may have heard, Bobbi, I've saved up a few bucks in my life. I have real estate investments across the country. As you know this resort isn't just a resort, but was once the location of a huge bunker that would house Congress in the event of a nuclear attack. The story leaked to the newspapers, and the government bagged the project in 1995 because it couldn't have a secret facility that everybody knew about. I bought the Greenbrier in 2008 and I live here. My wife, Estelle, died on 9/11. She was at a meeting in the North tower when the plane hit."

So, he's single, she thought, pushing the idea out of her head.

"And why did you buy it? It must be quite a challenge to run a resort," Bobbi aked.

"I didn't buy it as a financial investment, although I've made a tidy profit every year since I acquired the place. I bought the Greenbrier for the bunker, which I'll show you in a little while. Okay, call me a survivalist nutjob, but I read the tea leaves and I read the newspapers, including the one you work for. There's a lot of crazy shit going on in the world, have you noticed?"

"Yes, Zeke, I think 'crazy shit' summarizes the world news accurately."

"I've been a history buff ever since I majored in history in college," Zeke said. "The thought kept plaguing me, what if there was a nuclear war? Besides the obvious loss of life and political turmoil, what becomes of our history? Would a nuclear war and maybe an electromagnetic pulse or EMP be the end of our past as well as our future? Would humanity survive, not just physically, but intellectually? That's where we come in. We're replicating as much of the data in the world as possible right here at the Greenbrier. Private corporations are happy for us to back up their stuff, and pay us a fee to do so, on the condition that any link is to their site, not ours. Those fees are a big part of our revenue stream. My dream is that this place will continue to exist hundreds of years into the future."

"But why can't people simply get on the Internet and Google a search string and get the information by themselves?"

"What you just said is based on the assumption that there *is* an Internet. We base our thinking on the assumption that the Internet no longer exists. We're the Web's backup, but we go beyond the Web. We have a team of 24 historian/journalists who spend their time memorializing the present, which will someday be the past. You'll meet these folks. They're all smarter than hell, and well paid. They also get to live at a beautiful resort. Hey, Bobbi, if you ever get tired of chasing headlines, just give me a call. You would immediately become the prettiest reporter at the Greenbrier."

She ignored his obvious flirtation. It didn't bother her, she just ignored it—for the time being.

"Zeke, you mentioned an EMP or an Electromagnetic Pulse explosion. Wouldn't that impact your equipment as well?"

"You're about to find out why I'm called paranoid, Bobbi. All of our servers are replicated in a deep underground storage bunker that's shielded by lead. I can't predict what would happen if we sustained a direct hit, but why would anybody want to waste a bomb on us? Remember, the government is longer here."

"So let me get this straight, Zeke. It's your mission to preserve the past, and the present as it becomes the past. And you call yourselves simply the Greenbrier?"

"No! Check this out. The Greenbrier is just a location. Our people, our organization, needed a name. One of our brainiacs came up with the idea a year ago that we should call ourselves *The Keepers of Time*. How cool is that, Bobbi? *The Keepers of Time*."

CHAPTER THIRTY TWO

President Reynolds asked (okay, ordered) Bill and me to stay close by. One of his aides arranged for us to stay at Blair House, the president's guest facility, across Pennsylvania Avenue from the White House. I asked and received permission for Jack and Bill's wife Magda to join us.

The four of us sat in a private dining room. Bill and I discussed our meeting with the president. We didn't worry about security clearances, because Bill and Magda knew more than we did.

"Tomorrow," I said, "will be the most important meeting of our lives. I believe that the President gets it. He's lost his skepticism of time travel, and I think we've convinced him that less than a year from now, the world as we know it will end. The upshot, of course, is that the country may have to go to war with Iran and North Korea. Reynolds is going to be spending a couple of days burning the phone lines with our allies. He's a persuasive guy, so I'm not worried about that."

"What *are* you worried about, Ashley?" Jack said.

"My colleagues in the military. We're not talking about a few air strikes—we're talking war, including ground troops. After Iraq and Afghanistan, the country has grown war-weary. But this is different. We're faced with a threat to the very existence of our country. Every politician is wary of using the phrase 'boots on the ground,' but it will need to happen."

"I assume that I won't be able to sit in," said Magda, "although I'd love to."

"That's correct Magda," I said. "I think President Reynolds is developing an ulcer over sharing Top Secret information with Bill, who not only lacks a security clearance, but he isn't even an American citizen. Although Jack is a reserve officer, he has Top Secret clearance. We know that West Virginia is part of the United States, but you need proof to show you were born here."

"We should hit the rack early," Jack said. "I don't think I'm exaggerating when I say that tomorrow is a big day."

"I'll entertain myself with the wonderful video selection on the TV in our room," said Magda, "while you folks are trying to keep the world from blowing up."

⚊⁺ ⁺⚊

A Marine guard escorted Jack, Bill, and me into the Oval Office. An aide then told us that we would adjourn to the cabinet room because of the large number of people in the meeting. I had never been in the cabinet room before. It's really just a large conference room, with extra floor space for reporters and photographers. But there would be no press coverage of this meeting.

General Randolph McCracken, Chairman of the Joint Chiefs of Staff was there, along with Bill Carlini, Director of the CIA, and our good old friend Buster, aka Agent Gamal Akhbar, super spy of super spies. Sarah Watson, FBI Director, sat next to Carlini. Also there was Jerome Goodkind, Army Chief of Staff, General

Mark Bellows, Commandant of the Marine Corps, General of the Air Force William Schmidt, and my old friend Admiral Roland Townsend, Chief of Naval Operations. The cast of characters alone announced that this would be a war meeting.

President Reynolds introduced Jack and me, although most in the room knew us. He then introduced the mystery guest, Bill Wellfleet. Reynolds gave a brief and accurate rundown of what we had discussed yesterday. The President was about to call on Bill, but he wanted to grab the attention of everyone in the room.

"Ladies and gentlemen, our country will soon come under nuclear attack, and the purpose of this meeting is to prevent it."

Reynolds poured himself a glass of water as he let his words seep in. This guy knows how to start a meeting, I thought.

"You've been briefed on this matter, but I'm going to give you a quick rundown on our guest, Bill Wellfleet," Reynolds said. "To eliminate the bullshit and get right to the point, Bill comes to us from the future, the year 2227. Yes, he's time traveled along with our friends Admiral Ashley Patterson and her husband, naval reserve officer, author, and famous journalist Jack Thurber. Bill Wellfleet is the leader of a group of people located at the old Greenbrier Resort in West Virginia, a place that was intended as the seat of government in case of a nuclear attack until a few years ago. The group that Bill leads is known as *The Keepers of Time*. They have a database that would put the FBI and CIA to shame. I said I'd get to the point. Bill tells us, from his vantage point in the future, that the United States will be attacked on April 12, 2018, just shy of a year from now. It's not an opinion; it's not something he seems to recall; it's an actual prediction based on hard evidence. I'll turn the meeting over to Bill. Oh, I know a few of you will be wondering if Bill has security clearance to be in this meeting. Well, if we take him at his word, he was born in West Virginia, in the United States. If he can document that, he's a natural American citizen. No, he does not have Top Secret clearance, but we'll have to sort that shit out later. Bill, please tell us what you know."

In the brief time I've known Bill Wellfleet, I was impressed by his calm demeanor, articulate speaking, and his sense of humor. Nothing about my impression of him changed at this meeting, except for one thing. When he gets angry, he takes no bullshit, as we'd see shortly. Bill gave us the rundown of what he told the President yesterday.

"So, yes," he summed up after a half hour talk, "on April 12, 2018, less than a year from now, the United States will be attacked by Iran and North Korea with nuclear weapons. Almost every major city, including Washington, D.C. and New York will be destroyed. Within a short time after the war, the United States will no longer exist as a country. The political map of the entire world will change as well."

"Mr. Wellfleet," said General Bellows, Commandant of the Marine Corps, with a look that can only be described as a sneer, "I've never been a fan of science fiction, so I have a hard time accepting nonsense. Are you really telling us that you've traveled here from the future?"

My gentle intellectual historian friend suddenly showed a side I didn't know he had. The table was arranged in a horseshoe, so he walked up to General Bellows, leaned over and put his hands on the surface in front of him. He drilled his eyes into Bellows.

"Here's the fact, general, like it or not. I've come from the future, 210 years into the future. I don't know what kind of novels you read, science fiction or not, nor do I care. To the extent you stop sharing your skepticism, is the extent to which this meeting can move forward. I come from the year 2227. Live with it."

Bellows is a distinguished combat veteran, with a chest full of ribbons to show for it. He looked like he'd just been shot.

Bill walked over to the video projector, after giving Bellows one last eye zing.

"Ladies and gentlemen, to summarize the evidence," Bill said, "I'll now show you written statements by representatives of the Iranian government as well as North Korea. These statements were taken years after the war was over, and after these people defected. To zero in on the point, you have to attack the Iranian uranium enrichment facility at Natanz and pulverize it. I'm not a military man, nor an explosives expert, but my research tells me that you should consider the 30,000 pound Massive Ordnance Penetrator or MOP, the GBU 57A/B. You then have to turn your attention to this building in Busan, North Korea." He pointed to the building on the screen. "It houses 135 nuclear bombs, including 85 from Iran. They purchased the other 50 on the black market after the Soviet Union fell. The weapons are destined for cargo ships bearing short-range ballistic missiles. North Korea will be the easy part—destroying the building that houses the bombs—although I express no opinion of what your ground forces will encounter."

"I'm sure there are questions," said the President.

"Can we have access to your database?" said Buster the spy.

"Of course," said Bill. "I've already given a hard drive to the President. I'll be available for any and all questions to interpret the data."

"This may not be relevant, Mr. Wellfleet," said Sarah Watson, "but I've always been fascinated by the Greenbrier. My husband and I took a golf vacation there a few years ago, before you acquired it. In my recent reading, I recall that the new owner is a man named Ezekiel Wellfleet. Is that a coincidence?"

"No it isn't Madam Secretary. Grandpa Zeke, as we call him, was indeed the founder of The *Keepers of Time*. He's my great, great—how many greats can you fit into 210 years—grandfather. Over the span of time, every leader of *The Keepers* has been a Wellfleet. It's been an immovable tradition. My nephew, Joshua Wellfleet, has taken over in my absence. When things calm down, I look forward to visiting the Greenbrier to meet Grandpa Zeke. It should be interesting. I'm a year older than him, after making a 210-year time adjustment."

"Let's get back on message, folks," said President Reynolds. "We've been talking about a future as if we're actually living it now. I'm going to ask Bill Wellfleet to explain to us just what his future looks like."

"Mr. President," said Wellfleet, "I'll defer to Admiral Patterson and her husband Jack. I believe they can give you a perspective that I can't."

Probably a good idea to hear about the future from Jack and me, but I was starting to get used to being back in the present. Have I mentioned that time travel sucks at times?

"Thanks, Bill.," I said. "I hope that between Jack and me we can give you folks a sense of what the future looks like. It's a combination of civilization that we're used to, as shown by *The Keepers*, and a grinding depravity that you would expect from dystopian literature. We saw a land, once known as the United States, that consisted of small political and geographic units they call towns. There was little organization and very little cooperation between the towns. They seemed to exist for the purpose of raiding and fending off raids. They had their farms and ranches, and some of them even had small manufacturing enterprises. For the most part these towns were bands of nomadic people held together by warlords."

"Can you give us a sense of how large the population was (or will be)?" CIA Director Carlini asked.

"You will find what I'm about to say shocking, Director Bill," I said, as I looked at my notes. "The world population right now in 2017 is estimated to be 7.3 billion people, with 326 million in the United States. According to Bill Wellfleet and the historians at *The Keepers*, the population of the world in 2227 is 900 million, with the former United States at 25 million. The world will shrink in the next 210 years. It was a combination of direct deaths from the nuclear war, followed by months and years of deaths from radiation poisoning and cancer, and probably worst of all, a sharp decline in fertility apparently the result of genetic mutations."

"What about day-to-day life?" said FBI Director Watson. "What was it like?"

"Two radical distinctions, Madam Director," I said. "In areas occupied by *The Keepers of Time* everyday life was busy and productive. In the towns, it was a totally different story. There was no such thing as football, baseball, or soccer, but there were stadiums. Each town had a stadium, some rudimentary, some just a set of bleachers."

"But if nobody played ball, what were the stadiums for?" Buster asked.

"The stadiums were for the new national pastime, except that there was no nation. The great pastime in all of the towns was gladiatorial combat. They would pit young people against one another in fights to the death. Most of the participants came from kidnappings of neighboring towns. It was a slave trade. The warlords used gladiatorial contests to keep the townspeople busy and satisfied, much as in ancient Rome. We were shown a video shot from a drone, of a contest that pitted two pretty young women against each other in a town that called itself the Eastern Empire. It was located in what is now Arlington, Virginia. We watched, horrified, as a young lady who was kidnapped from the Greenbrier, was beheaded before our eyes. Jack and Bill can tell you my reaction. I ran to the bathroom and threw up."

The people in the room were visibly shaken. Most had their faces in their hands.

"Could you describe those towns as enemies of *The Keepers,* and have they threatened or attacked?" said General McCracken.

"Yes, general," I said. "Any town could always be considered an enemy, but most of them knew not to threaten *The Keepers* because they maintain a strong security force. But there have been attacks over the years, including a major one while we were there. I was at sea putting my crew through training exercises when I received a call from Bill Wellfleet, telling me that a column of 100 armed vehicles was headed toward the Greenbrier. I immediately launched eight sorties of F18s and attacked the column. We destroyed it. Then I steamed south to get closer to Arlington, the site of the pompously named town, the Eastern Empire. My objective was to degrade or destroy the town's ability to make war. Bill Wellfleet and the other folks at the Greenbrier provided us with targeting information from the *Keepers'* database. I took out their command and control center, which was a large house. I also attacked their ammunition depot, and a military barracks. I personally targeted the gladiatorial stadium and attacked it with incendiary rockets and bombs. We destroyed the structure in minutes."

"Yesss," yelled my friend Admiral Townsend, as he slapped his hand on the table. "Do I know how to pick a strike group commander or not? Way to go, Ashley!"

"I then sent a Marine detachment ashore to tend to the survivors, most of whom were slaves captured by the town. Bill Wellfleet told me that he was dispatching vehicles to bring the survivors to the Greenbrier. A couple of days later I personally observed how the survivors were treated, given housing, and generally welcomed warmly by the *Keepers* folks."

"This may seem like a stickler of a point, admiral," said General McCracken, Chairman of the Joint Chiefs, "but you couldn't have had any rules of engagement for attacking those people."

I almost laughed.

"General, I found myself as commander of Carrier Strike Group 2311, which had suddenly been reduced to one ship, the *Reagan*. As the operational commander my job was to observe the reality around me, to make command decisions, and to act on them. I discovered that we had a good friend and ally, *The Keepers of Time*, which found itself under attack. I stand by my decision to defend *The Keepers* and to destroy its enemy."

I guess I said the right thing. The room erupted in applause, led by the President himself. General McCracken stood and applauded.

"Okay, folks," said President Reynolds, "we're going to take a short break. Lunch will be served right here in the interest of time. We have a lot more work to do."

CHAPTER THIRTY THREE

Seth Lombardi, editor-in-chief of *The Daily Keeper*, and first deputy of *The Keepers*, stood before the capacity audience in the main theater of the Greenbrier.

"Ladies and gentlemen, it gives me great pleasure and pride to introduce our new leader, the new *Samah* if you will, Joshua Wellfleet."

The crowd stood and gave Wellfleet a thunderous applause. As the applause died down, Joshua approached the microphone.

"My aunt and uncle, Bill and Magda Wellfleet, made a noble decision, one that we'd expect of them. They have decided to travel back in time with Admiral Patterson and her ship to try to undo some of the mayhem of the past 210 years. I was on the boat that Admiral Patterson gave to us, and I saw the ship disappear off Long Island, presumably through the wormhole we've heard so much about. They are now in the year 2017. I only hope that they will see fit to return to us through the wormhole at some time in the future. I stand in front of you folks feeling terribly humbled. I'm only 23 years old, and I do not deserve the position you've trusted me with. And you've trusted me with this position because of one fact: My name is Wellfleet. So I stand before you and ask you to reconsider. There are better leaders here than me, and I'm asking you to make a different choice."

Seth Lombardi approached the microphone.

"May I, Joshua?" he said, pointing to the microphone. Joshua nodded.

"Over 210 years ago a man named Ezekiel Wellfleet made a decision of historical importance. He founded *The Keepers of Time*, right here at the Greenbrier. Since then, every single leader of our community has been a blood descendent of his, every single leader has been a Wellfleet. God knows, we're not royalty, far from it, but as the preservers of time and history, we believe in tradition, and one tradition has never been broken; our leader has always been a Wellfleet. Over the years, we have had a few problems with the tradition. About 100 years ago, if I recall from my reading, we chose a two-year-old as our leader."

Everyone laughed at one of the more entertaining episodes of *The Keepers'* history.

"Little Randolph Wellfleet needed a bit of help, to say the least, but he grew up to be one of the finest leaders we've ever had. Randolph Wellfleet is credited with one of the greatest quotations from our long history: '*The Keepers of Time* works, because we *want* it to work.' And that is as true today as the day Randolph said it. Joshua, you will succeed because we *want you to succeed*. Welcome leader, *Samah*, the latest of a long wonderful line of Wellfleets."

He handed the microphone back to Joshua, who stood and looked out at the crowd.

"I won't let you down," Joshua said.

CHAPTER THIRTY FOUR

After lunch, President Reynolds resumed the meeting.
"Thanks to our new friend, Bill Wellfleet, we now have the evidence to support a conclusion that Iran and North Korea intend to attack us, but it's not enough. I have to get on the phone and round up our allies, which is similar to herding cats. What we're missing is actual on-site evidence that I can use to convince our allies to go to war. We now have knowledge of something we never knew before, the enhanced uranium enrichment facility near Natanz in Iran. But we don't have a precise location."

Bill Wellfleet raised his hand.

"Mr. President," Wellfleet said, "I'm sorry if I gave too cursory an overview, but I do have an exact location."

Bill looked at his notes.

"The new facility at Natanz is exactly 1000 yards to the northeast—I have the precise coordinates—and it's 300 feet below the level of the existing facility."

The President looked at CIA Director Carlini.

"What can you do with that information, Bill? Can the CIA corroborate it so I can hit Iran with an ultimatum?"

Carlini looked at Buster.

"Naturally I have a few of my guys inside," Buster said. "Spies are trained to look for things they don't know about. But once we know what to look for, especially if we have a location, it's a piece of cake. I can have one of my moles corroborate what Mr. Wellfleet told us. It will be dangerous and it will take some time, but we can do it. Figure about two weeks, maybe less."

"Once I have that information," the President said, "I can go to our allies and convince them to close ranks. Then I'll go to Iran and say, 'let our inspectors in or I'll blow the shit out of your country.' I never think of the Iranians as particularly rational opponents, but they're not insane. They'll buckle. Are you sure you can get us the corroborating intelligence, Buster?"

"Yes, sir. I can get it," Buster said.

"And now for North Korea. We know of 135 bombs and we know exactly where they are. I have to negotiate with China to help me talk to their unwanted 'ally.' I've always had the impression that China looks at North Korea as an uncle who has suddenly inherited his juvenile delinquent nephew. I can get China to look the other way when I deliver an ultimatum to North Korea. I know what I have to do, and we all know what *we* have to do"

The meeting was over. I'd always been impressed with President Reynolds. He's one of the most thoughtful people I'd ever met, and also one of the most decisive. If the country ever needed decisiveness, it's now. I'd hate to be in the President's shoes right now.

CHAPTER THIRTY FIVE

"Bobbi, I'm so glad that you could stay at the Greenbrier last night," Zeke Wellfleet said, as they had breakfast in a private dining room.

"It was my pleasure, Zeke. This place is beautiful. I can't wait to write my article. I think it's safe to say that you and your *The Keepers of Time* have impressed me. I'm not supposed to say something like that to a person I'm interviewing for an article, but it's the truth. I think you people are on to something big, something big *and* important. Maybe it's the journalist in me, but I love what you folks are doing—preserving the truth."

"I hope you'll come back here from time to time. Maybe you can track our project and write follow-up articles for the *Times*," Zeke said.

She smiled at him. Damn, this guy is handsome, she thought.

"I'd love to come back. I have to admit something. People call you a nut, but I don't see it that way at all, now that I've met you. But if you *are* a nut, I think you're the cutest nut I've ever met."

"Are you flirting with me, Bobbi?"

"I'm afraid I am. God, I'm embarrassed, but I find you a very attractive guy. You're disarmingly frank about what's going on here, you talk straight, and there's another thing I've noticed. You have beautiful eyes. Sorry, I feel like a complete jerk. Here I am, a reporter for *The New York Times*, and I'm flirting with the man I'm interviewing."

Zeke put his elbows on the table and his face in his hands.

"Are you blushing, Zeke?"

"Yes, I suppose I am. Since my Estelle died, I've thrown myself into making this place a historical reality. There are plenty of good-looking women around here, but I'll admit that there's something about you that, well, makes me blush. Hey, you mentioned that you have another assignment to get to, but could I convince you to stay one more night. We're having our first showing of *The King and I* in our main theater. I'd like you to be my special guest. I think you'll find our theatrical productions are as good as the other stuff we do around here."

"Are you asking me out on a date, Zeke?"

"Yes."

"Well, I accept. I do have another assignment, but it can wait. I think the more time I spend here, the better my article will be. Did I just speak as a serious journalist?"

"Yes, Bobbi, you did sound like a serious journalist, because that's what you are. You also sounded like a lady who would enjoy another evening of my company. Am I being off base by saying that?"

"No, you're not, Zeke. I'm really happy that I got this assignment."

CHAPTER THIRTY SIX

Time flies when you're scared out of your mind. I can't believe that we've been back here in the 21st Century for almost a year. Today is April 1, 2018, 12 days away from what we thought would be a nuclear Armageddon.

I voted for William Reynolds when he ran for president. As a military officer, I couldn't actively support him but I wanted to. After I've seen him in action over the past few months, I'm convinced he's one of the greatest presidents of modern times. He pulled off a diplomatic coup and averted a certain war—a nuclear war.

Reynolds, calmly and methodically, visited with all of our major allies and convinced them, based on the CIA confirmation of what Bill Wellfleet predicted, that we had to present a united front. He even got Vladimir Putin to see things his way.

Reynolds insisted that he meet personally with Iran's top leadership, and not leave it to lower level negotiations. He took me and a few other advisors with him to the talks. When he presented his findings to the Iranian government, he refused to be drawn into negotiations, although the mullahs wanted to talk about removing further sanctions.

"I'm not here to negotiate," Reynolds said, "I'm here to tell you what we expect you to do, and you have exactly 48 hours. If you don't allow our inspection team, accompanied by high level people from the UN, into your enrichment facility at Natanz, we well bomb you into dust. If we run low on bombs, we'll be followed by Germany, France, England, and Russia. Yes, even Russia. You have brought the world to the brink of war, and you will be punished for it. I repeat, sir, you have 48 hours."

Holy shit, I thought. Reynolds is one tough guy.

Iran backed down completely in the face of Reynold's immoveable stance. We inspected the new secret facility near Natanz, and it was just as Bill Wellfleet said, a bomb-making plant. We reimposed sanctions, harsh sanctions, and Iran capitulated, with no choice but to do so.

Reynolds then turned his attention to North Korea. He did this by negotiating directly with the Chinese. There is no such thing as negotiating with North Korea. He convinced the Chinese that on a dock by a harbor in North Korea, was a warehouse containing 135 nuclear bombs. Another ultimatum, but, because of Reynold's brilliant diplomacy, the ultimatum was *delivered by the Chinese.* The only concession he had to make was that the weapons would become property of China. He saw no problem with that, because China was already a nuclear power, and 135 more bombs wouldn't change the status quo a bit. Kim Jong-un backed down, and allowed the weapons to be taken away. He had no choice. China feared a nuclear war as much as the United States and its allies, and they made it clear to the Korean dictator that he had overplayed his hand—and stood alone.

The nuclear war of April 12, 2018 had been averted.

⇒⇇ ⇉⇐

On April 13, 2018, Jack and I had dinner with Bill and Magda Wellfleet at an elegant restaurant in Georgetown. President Reynolds had ordered us to stay close by until the big date passed, which, thank God, it did.

"You folks know what Magda and I want to do," Bill said. "President Reynolds basically forbade us from doing this until now, now that the horrible date has passed."

"Of course, Bill," I said. "You want to visit the Greenbrier and meet Grandpa Zeke. We'd love to be with you, but I understand that you want to see him alone. I'd love to be a fly on the wall when you two meet. You've had a lot of amazing experiences in your life, but this will probably top them all. I have one big question. Will you and Magda stay here in 2018 or will you return to 2227?"

"The answer to that question, Ashley, depends on what we encounter at the Greenbrier. I have no idea what we'll see, but we won't make our decision until after that meeting."

CHAPTER THIRTY SEVEN

My name may be Wellfleet, but I'm not sure how they'll react to that at the Greenbrier. Magda and I decided to arrive unannounced at the Greenbrier, checking first to make sure that Grandpa Zeke would be there.

Before we left the Greenbrier of the future, my colleagues insisted that Magda and I bring some tradeable assets with us. They gave us a gold bar, which weighed 400 troy ounces, or about 33 pounds. Jack set us up to meet his banker, who had the gold assayed. Our little gold bar was worth over 5-million dollars in 2018. Jack's banker happily set us up with taxpayer identification numbers, a bank account, and credit cards. At least we wouldn't be a financial burden to our new friends.

With some of our new "walking around money," we rented a Mercedes, the same model that I drove 210 years from now. The drive would take a bit over four hours from Washington, We left at 8 a.m. planning to arrive at noon, in time for lunch, always a good way to break the ice. It was a beautiful mid-April day, warm and sunny. We enjoyed our drive. One thing we both found shocking was all the cars on the road, and the sheer number of people everywhere we looked.

We drove up the entrance road to the Greenbrier. I stopped the car about 50 yards from the entrance so we could take in the view, the 210-year-old view. Magda took a photo out of her purse, and we compared what we saw to the place we used to live. It looked almost the same.

"You know," I said, "one thing I never thought much about was the landscaping work at the Greenbrier. Obviously our gardeners are historians as well. This looks like the place we left 210 years from now."

A young man in a smart-looking uniform met us at the door and put our bags on a cart.

"Welcome to the Greenbrier," he said. "Ever been here before?"

"Well, sort of," Magda said. The poor kid didn't know what to make of that. He just looked at her with a furrowed brow.

We entered the main lobby—it could have been yesterday. I stopped walking and touched Magda's elbow.

"Look who's here," I said.

A tall pretty blond wearing an expensive spring business suit approached us. She had a clipboard under one arm. We recognized her from photos on our database.

"Welcome to the Greenbrier," she said, with a broad smile. "I'm Roberta Simmons. Please call me Bobbi. I'm on host duty today, but usually I'm assigned to the history room. I'm a journalist by trade. And who are you folks?"

Okay, I thought. It was time to break the ice, except I felt I was about to do it with a sledgehammer.

"I'm Bill Wellfleet and this is my wife, Magda."

"Wellfleet?" Bobbi said. "My fiancé, Zeke Wellfleet, is the owner of this place. Could you be related?"

"Yes, Bobbi," I said, "I'm Zeke Wellfleet's distant grandson."

"Grandson!" she yelled. "But you look the same age as Zeke. How old are you?"

"I'm 43."

"My God, you're a year older than him. I think you must be confused about something."

Bobbi had the look on her face of someone about to call security.

"I'd love to explain everything, Bobbi. We used to live here. May I suggest that the four of us have lunch? It will be an experience that the journalist in you will never forget."

She picked up a phone off the counter. "Jimmy, I need you to spell me in the lobby for a couple of hours. Thanks, pal." She hit another number.

"Zeke, honey, get your butt down here. I want you to meet a couple of fascinating people. Prepare to have your mind blown."

⇥+ +⇤

Within five minutes a guy in an expensive Savile Row suit walked into the lobby. All of my reading and all of the photos I'd seen of him came back to me. He was known as one of the most dapper dressers in the world, or at least in West Virginia.

He walked up to us and extended his hand, smiling but with a slight look of confusion on his face.

He looked into my face, and I looked at him. Oh, my God, after all of the years, we bore a definite resemblance to each other. I saw Bobbi looking back and forth at us, her mouth open.

"Zeke," Bobbi said, "this guy, sorry, this gentleman, says his name is Bill Wellfleet, and he says that you're his distant grandfather. I told you I'd blow your mind, and I think I just did."

Zeke was speechless. From everything I'd ever read about him, this was a rare affliction. He has a reputation as a nonstop talker.

He held out his hand gesturing to a separate room off to the right. Oh my God, I thought, it's still the private dining room.

We sat. Zeke stared.

"I can't even begin to form any questions," Zeke said. "Maybe my favorite journalist here can think of something."

Bobbi just shook her head.

"Okay, folks, let me take it from the top" I said, "or the bottom, or wherever. I'm sure you read about the two-hour disappearance of the *USS Ronald Reagan* a while ago."

"Sure," Zeke said. "It was one of the wildest news stories any of us ever read. Some people think it had something to do with time travel. But how does that involve you and Magda?"

"Magda and I hitched a ride on the *Reagan* when it returned to the present time. We come from the year 2227, over 200 years from now. I'm the leader of *The Keepers of Time,* the 2227 edition. Zeke, I'm not throwing out any overblown compliments here, but you are the most important man in the world. You started *The Keepers,* and you succeeded beyond your wildest dreams. Yes, in 2227, *The Keepers* were just that, the keepers of civilization. And you were the original *Samah.*"

"*Samah?*" Zeke said, laughing. "You still use that term?"

"We actually do, Zeke, but not often. With all of the research at our disposal, you'd think we know where the term comes from, but it's still a mystery to us. We think it means leader, but we don't know the origin of the word. Do you know where the word *Samah* comes from, Zeke?"

Zeke roared with laughter. He glanced out the window and stood.

"Come here," he said as he walked to the window. "Behold *The Samah.*"

He pointed to a truck in the driveway. The inscription on the side read, "Samah Plumbing and Heating." Zeke laughed again. "I'm glad the truck was here today."

"A couple of years ago a few of us were having cocktails on a Friday evening. One guy suggested that I should have an important sounding title. The guy pointed at that truck. I immediately adopted my formal title as *Samah*. You may notice that we don't take ourselves too seriously around here."

"I've read a mountain of information about time travel," Zeke said, "and I'm convinced that it's true, a strange phenomenon maybe, but true. Now you're telling us that you have traveled here from 210 years into the future? Hey, Bobbi, shouldn't you be taking notes?"

Bobbi nodded her head and began jotting things down.

"You obviously know a lot about Zeke and me," Bobbi said. "You may also know that I'm a black belt in karate. So let me advise you, Bill, if you ever call me grandma I shall break your nose."

We all laughed. Bobbi Simmons (soon to be Bobbi Wellfleet) was just as charming as everything I had read about her.

"Okay, Bill," Zeke said, "for the purpose of this conversation, I'm going to assume that I haven't flipped out and that you're telling us the truth. Now let me ask a few questions. You say that you're the leader of *The Keepers* over 200 years from now. Where are they located?"

"Right here, Zeke, here at the Greenbrier—and yes we still call it that. Magda, please show Zeke and Bobbi some photos. This, you may be shocked to know, is what the Greenbrier will look like in 210 years. We've done a pretty good job of preservation, no? Our landscaping people pay a lot of attention to preserving the original look of this place. Oh, you may also notice the way Magda and I are dressed, and the way we talk."

"I have noticed that," said Bobbi. "If this story is true that you came here from over 200 years into the future, I'd expect you people to be dressed like aliens and speak a strange language. But you're just like any other guests, well a bit better dressed maybe."

"We've taken Zeke's philosophy and kept to it," I said. "As *The Keepers of Time*, we're preservationists, and that means preserving as much of reality as it existed in this time, including clothing and speech."

"Bill," said Bobbi, "sorry, but the pain-in-the-ass reporter in me is starting to wake up. I have a simple but important question. Why did you come here?"

"We came here to prevent what almost happened yesterday. In the reality we came from, the day April 12, 2018 was the day the world ended in a nuclear conflagration."

"Oh, my God. It's been all over the news. President Reynolds managed to prevent Iran and North Korea from starting a nuclear war. Yes, it was supposed to be yesterday. But what does that have to do with you?"

"Remember, Zeke, we're *The Keepers*. We knew everything about yesterday, and a lot more into the immediate future. I hope I'm not violating any state secrets here, but we gave Reynolds and his intelligence people the facts about what Iran and North Korea intended, a lot more than you know right now. We know this because we're *The Keepers*. And it's all thanks to a guy named Zeke Wellfleet, a man who a lot of people dismissed as an eccentric. If it weren't for you, Zeke, and what we've inherited from you, the world as we knew it would not exist."

"But Bill," Bobbi said, "didn't you say that in the year you came from, the history actually did include the war, the one that was supposed to happen yesterday?"

"That's correct, Bobbi, we come from a place that includes a history of a nuclear war. From what I'm learning about time travel, we find ourselves in a different version of reality."

"But what happened to the Greenbrier, to *The Keepers*? In the post-nuclear war version of history?" Zeke asked.

"Just what you intended, Zeke, nothing. Partially because no bombs falling anywhere near here. No fallout, no shock waves, nothing. The Greenbrier got away free, but even if the war got closer, *The Bunker* would have survived."

"You know about *The Bunker?*" Zeke said.

"Of course we know about *The Bunker.* Do I have to remind you, Magda and I are part of *The Keepers? The Bunker* is one of our reasons to exist."

"What happened to the rest of the world?" Bobbi said.

"You may want to finish lunch before I answer that, Bobbi. We have a video to show you of a talk I prepared for the crew of the *Reagan,* explaining the war and its impact over the next 210 years. But I'll just give you a summary. New York, Washington, D.C, Chicago and Los Angeles were completely destroyed by direct nuclear blasts. After about five years, any remnant of the United States died as well. Where we come from, the outposts of *The Keepers*—and yes, you'll be happy to know there are a few—are the only remains of what you would call civilization. The rest of what was once America became lawless places called towns, run by warlords. They subsist by raiding neighboring towns. Their only form of entertainment are gladiatorial fights held in stadiums build for that purpose. The gladiators are slaves captured from raids. So, yes, Zeke, it's a fine organization that you've built."

"But now that you've prevented the nuclear, doesn't that change history?" Zeke asked.

"Yes it does, Zeke, and none of knows how."

Zeke and Bobbi took us on a tour of the Greenbrier. Although the place is our home, we had never visited the 2018 version. Because Magda and I knew the history of the Greenbrier intimately, we helped to conduct the tour, indicating places that were changed and showing them where additions were built. After we toured the entire facility, the four of us walked the beautiful grounds, having a strange conversation that only time travelers can appreciate. Suddenly, Zeke stopped and turned to us.

"What became of Bobbi and me in the alternate history you know so much about?"

"Zeke," I said," you have just asked a question that I shouldn't answer, but in your case I will, because my answer will make you happy. As you know, you and Bobbi will get married in two months. From the history that I know, you passed away at the age of 96 after telling a joke at a dinner. You sat down, closed your eyes, and moved on. Bobbi died in her sleep a few years later at the age of 101. You had four great kids, one of whom was *The Samah* when you died. Your 20 grandchildren also became an intimate part of the Greenbrier. You left the world a great legacy, Zeke. So that's the history that we know. What we don't know is what the future will look like now that history has changed."

Zeke and Bobbi hugged. Bobbi wept quietly.

"Bill, you're not planning on leaving us are you?" Zeke said. "Stay here at the Greenbrier. Live out your lives in a place you love. From what you've told us, you don't have any immediate relatives in the year you came from, no kids, no siblings. Stay with us. Magda can be our theater director, a position I've been thinking about for a while. You, Bill, will be our chief historian, our most important job. I'll pay you well, and you'll have free housing. Welcome to the past. So how about building a future here?"

"Bill, that's something that Magda and I need to discuss. The idea of working for the legendary Ezekiel Wellfleet is appealing, to say the least. Also, we feel like we're home."

"That's because you *are* home," Bobbi said. "You two stay put. You belong here."

"One big question, folks," Zeke said. "Is there anything at the Greenbrier that could use immediate improvement?"

"Security," both Magda and I blurted out. "You need to beef up security immediately."

"Security?" Zeke said. "Sure we have a couple of guards on staff to handle the occasionally unruly guest, but why bother with a lot of security. Hell, in the alternate history you discussed, the Greenbrier wasn't even a target in the war. We love to have guests and visitors roaming around. Hey that's our mission, to share information and history."

"Zeke, remember, we come from a lawless place in the future. We kept ourselves together by having a strong security force to repel attackers. Yes, I know, that's the distant future, but my reading tells me that the world has some tough customers who like nothing more than death and destruction here in the 21st Century. Do I have to remind you of 9/11?"

"I hear you, Bill, why would anybody would want to harm to the Greenbrier or *The Keepers*?"

CHAPTER THIRTY EIGHT

"Would you like a cup of tea, Mustaffa?" Muhammed Sidduq said to his second in command, Mustaffa Islama. Sidduq had just assumed the mantle as the head of the Islamic State, also known as ISIS, the Islamic State in Iraq and Syria. Even though it was founded in 1999, the term has become as familiar as al-Qaeda. It's also known as ISIL, for the Islamic State in the Levant, the Levant being a region including Iraq, Syria, Eastern Libya, and the Sinai Peninsula of Egypt. Sidduq's predecessor as head of the Islamic State had recently been killed by a drone missile strike on his headquarters. The two men met in a small one-story stucco building on the outskirts of Raqqa, Syria, the unofficial capital of the Islamic State.

"Mustaffa, the idiot Shiites of Iran have performed their usual buffoonery. They actually planned to wage a nuclear war against the United States and its allies. If they wanted to commit suicide, so be it, but why drag the rest of our brothers with them? Praise be to Allah that their plans were stopped. The way to the kingdom of Allah requires patience. It requires an Islamic State, which is exactly what we have formed. The Islamic State will prevail over the infidels, but it will take time. An 'End of Days' plan such as Iran was about to launch would have set us back hundreds of years."

"Yes, Muhammed, we are fortunate that their insane plan didn't work. Where do you see us going now?"

"Our plan of death by a thousand cuts is working. It's working slowly, as it must, but it *is* working. The martyrs who gave their lives in Paris a couple of years ago are a perfect example. Since then we have attacked hundreds of soft targets all over the heathen world. We have struck New York, Rome, Madrid, London, and Paris again. People are afraid to shop, to gather in crowds, or even to take public transportation. We are targeting the infidel in places he would least expect it, and we are winning."

"Do you have any idea that perhaps we should try something new, Muhammed?"

"Yes, I do, Mustaffa. There is a place in West Virginia in a town called White Sulphur Springs. It's called the Greenbrier, a resort where the infidels gather to frolic. The facility includes a large bunker carved into the side of a hill. The United States government once had a contract to relocate its leadership to the Greenbrier in the event of a nuclear war, and they chose the Greenbrier because of its hardened security. They abandoned the project after a newspaper report made it public. The entire facility, including the resort and the bunker, is now owned by a wealthy infidel named Ezekiel Wellfleet. He has formed an organization that calls itself *The Keepers of Time.* Their purpose is to preserve and protect the records of history. The facility includes a massive array of computers and assorted technology. Just as our brothers in the Taliban, we have targeted many ancient monuments, insults to the holy name of Allah. As the infidels bow before craven images, they also bow in idolatry to their 'history,' as if infidel history is at all important."

"But Muhammed, for the past few years we have concentrated on 'soft targets,' places and gatherings that we knew in advance were not secure. Surely this Greenbrier place must have a huge amount of security to protect itself."

"That is exactly why I'm choosing it as a target, Mustaffa. I visited the place a year ago. You would be amazed at its lack of security. They openly invite tourists and curiosity seekers and happily show them their work. I only saw two uniformed guards, and they weren't even wearing guns. Mustaffa, the Greenbrier and *The Keepers of Time* are ripe targets for the vengeance of Allah."

"You have convinced me, sir. As you speak, I wonder why we never thought of this before. But of course that is why you are our leader. Please give me the outline of your plans and I shall begin to contact our brothers to make preparations."

"As I said, Mustaffa, security will not be a problem. But to execute the plan the right way will require careful preparation and coordination between different groups of fighters. If we organize it properly, with enough weaponry and explosives, we will have a major impact on this rat hole of infidel history. Our plan should include martyrs in suicide bomb vests, as well as a large number of brothers with guns."

"I shall begin preparations immediately, Muhammed."

CHAPTER THIRTY NINE

April 12, 2018 came and went without a nuclear war, thanks to the input from our friend from the future, Bill Wellfleet, and thanks to the brilliant diplomacy of President Reynolds. I can't believe that I've been in Washington for almost a year. I was given an office in the White House as Special Naval Advisor to the President. Jack had no problem keeping himself busy with his writing assignments. I had been temporarily relieved of command of Carrier Strike Group 2311. The group was deployed to the Persian Gulf under command of Admiral William Richardson during the Iranian crisis. The President, God bless him, made sure that my record showed temporary relief from command because of my White House assignment. He didn't want my service record to show that I was relieved of command because I lost an aircraft carrier for a couple of hours. I was busy packing the small amount of items from my office, when the president himself walked in and handed me an envelope. Instinctively, I snapped to attention.

"Read it, Ashley," he said. "I think you'll like what you see."

I opened the envelope, trying to keep my hands from shaking.

The White House

April 14, 2018
FROM: President William Reynolds
TO: Vice Admiral Ashley Patterson

Dear Admiral Patterson:

Because of your exemplary service to the United States of America and the United States Navy, I am pleased to offer you the position as Superintendent of the United States Naval Academy.

Your courageous leadership and actions have brought pride to our country, and I'm sure that your position at Annapolis will inspire the future officers of the United States Navy.

Very truly yours,

William Reynolds, President, the United States of America With all of the crazy shit I've been through in my career, you'd think that I could take anything in stride. Didn't happen. I cried.

Reynolds gave me a bear hug, then looked into my eyes.

"Ashley, you're one of the finest military leaders I've ever met. I know that you've wanted this position, and I'm confident that you will bring the usual Ashley Patterson excellence to the job. I'm not going to wish you luck, because you always make your own luck. Give my best to Jack."

I went to our apartment in Georgetown. Jack wasn't there yet, which was fine by me. I wanted to surprise him when he walked in the door. When Jack walked in I wrapped my arms around his neck and we kissed.

"Now that's what I call a greeting, admiral. Are you excited about something or just happy to see me?"

I handed him a photograph of a house, a beautiful 17,000 square foot Beaux-Arts style mansion, the Buchanan House, the home of the Superintendent of the United States Naval Academy.

"What's this?" Jack said.

"Our new digs." I handed him the letter from the President.

Jack is a big guy, at 6'3." He picked me up in his arms and squeezed me.

"This is fabulous, baby. It's what you've always wanted."

"And my ass won't get deployed all over the world. We can actually be together. Me and my honey."

We hugged again.

"I'm so proud of you, babe," Jack said. "Hey, let's go out and celebrate."

We walked to our favorite French restaurant in Georgetown, a small quiet place that's great for conversation. We were shown to a table in the corner. Heavy drapes adorned the walls of the restaurant, adding to its quiet. Only two other couples were seated. Candlelight added to its warmth. I found myself thinking that the beautiful place came close to being wiped away by nuclear bombs. I took a deep breath, and let one word bathe my thoughts—peace.

"Jack, I almost forgot to tell you. I got a call from Bill Wellfleet. As you know he and Magda are at the Greenbrier. I can't imagine what his reaction must have been when he met Zeke Wellfleet. He invited us to stay for a few days. I have plenty of leave time coming so let's do it."

"Sounds great," Jack said. "Tell me if I'm wrong, but I think you take a proprietary interest in the Greenbrier since you saved it from being attacked."

"You're right, Jack. For some strange reason I still feel like I need to protect the place."

CHAPTER FORTY

J ack and I headed to the Greenbrier. It's hard to explain how I felt, and Jack said the same thing. The place had been such a focus of our lives for 15 strange days in the far future. Now we're going to see it as it exists in 2018.

"Holy shit (there I go again with my foul mouth). This place looks just like we saw it 210 years from now. *The Keepers* take their name seriously."

A bellman came out to greet us.

"Welcome to the Greenbrier folks. Been here before?"

"Yes, quite a bit," I said.

"When?" the bellman asked, being friendly.

"I don't recall," I said. Why freak the kid out, right?

We were escorted into the main lobby, which we knew so well. I couldn't believe that the room looked almost exactly like it did in 2227. Bill Wellfleet almost ran over to greet us.

"Come into the private dining room. There's somebody I want you to meet."

Bill escorted us into the dining room as if he owned the place. Well, doesn't he?

"Ashley and Jack, let me introduce Grandpa Zeke, a guy who's a bit younger than I am. And this lovely lady is Bobbi Simmons, Zeke's fiancé."

"Remember, Bill, don't call me grandma," Bobbi said with a smile At 3 p.m. Zeke suggested that we have a tour before dinner. As history recorded, Zeke was a charming guy. He spoke non-stop, pausing only to crack an occasional joke. Jack and I were amazed at the resemblance between Zeke and Bill. The Wellfleet line has strong genes, I thought. They took us through the entire *Bunker*, with Bill reminding us of the differences between now and 2227. Maybe I just couldn't shake my training, but I looked at everything from a military perspective, not as a vacationing guest. I couldn't get security out of my mind. In 2018, the constant threat we live with is terrorism. ISIS and al Qaeda love to attack soft targets, and often pick those targets for their symbolic value. What could be more symbolic than a resort that also served as a repository of history?

After our tour, we went back to the private dining room, which also looked exactly like it did in 2227.

Bill held up his glass and proposed a toast.

"To Admiral Ashley Patterson and her husband Jack," Bill said, "two of the greatest friends *The Keepers* have ever known. Along with the crew of the *USS Ronald Reagan*, they kept us safe."

Jack stood.

"And I would like to propose a toast to Ashley as well," Jack said. "I'm proud to announce that my beautiful wife is the next Superintendent of the United States Naval Academy."

They all applauded loudly. For a long time now, Jack and I have thought of Bill and Magda Wellfleet as good friends. In our brief time together, we felt the same way about Zeke and Bobbi.

"I'll make sure to get you folks tickets to the Army-Navy Game."

"Well, since we still have more champagne, let *me* propose a toast," Zeke said. "I'm delighted to announce that my grandchildren,

Bill and Magda, have decided to stay with us in the present time. Bill is our new chief historian and Magda is now our theater director. Long live *The Keepers of Time!*"

We all applauded. I couldn't have been happier that Bill and Magda would be staying on in their past. Our dinner conversation was wonderful. Talking to two leaders of an organization who are separated by 210 years is a rare gift.

"I have a question folks," Zeke said, "I'm a big believer in first impressions. You've seen the Greenbrier, a place that you've visited before in the distant future. So, here's my question. What's your first impression of the place? Please give us your honest gut impression."

He looked at me.

"A target," I said.

CHAPTER FORTY ONE

Jack and I stood on the huge porch of the Buchanan House as the moving truck pulled up. I had already taken over as Superintendent of the United States Naval Academy, but today was the official day that we moved into the superintendent's quarters. The place came fully furnished, so we had put most of our belongings in storage. The house was built in 1906, and was 17,000 square feet with 34 rooms. A large green awning adorned the front of the house, with smaller awnings surrounding the place. A pretty insane waste of taxpayer money to house two people, if you ask me, but it did serve for important receptions and ceremonial functions as well as a place for us to live. We didn't own it, of course, but we fell in love with the house. The walls included memorabilia and antique paintings, most of historical naval subjects. The mansion also sported 10 chimneys. To the left of the house loomed the green dome of the Chapel, one of the more iconic structures on the grounds of the academy.

Buchanan House was named for Civil War Admiral Franklin Buchanan. Only problem is that he was a *Confederate* admiral. I wondered when the demands of political correctness would re-name the house.

Jack and I had coffee and a light breakfast in the main dining room, taking a break from our normal routine of starting our day with breakfast in a diner.

"So you've been on the job for a month now, hon," said Jack. "How do you like it?"

"Jack, sometimes I feel like I'm a dorm supervisor. Hey, I don't want to sound old, but a lot of what's going on here irks the shit out of me. Hell, I graduated from this place just under 20 years ago, but things have changed. In one month I've seen more complaints of sexual misconduct cross my desk than I'd like to believe. Now, look at it this way, if you put together a few hundred young and physically fit men and women, do you somehow remove the word 'horny' from the vocabulary? Don't get me wrong, if any woman is sexually assaulted, and I mean assaulted, not consensual sex, the perpetrator should be punished, severely. But a lot of what I'm seeing is just vindictive bullshit from somebody who was jilted. In one case I'm looking at, a woman complained that she was sexually assaulted 15 times, and she brought formal complaints against all 15 of her fellow midshipmen, including five men who were away on training exercises at the time of the alleged incidents. I wanted to mark her file, 'vindictive slut,' but of course I didn't."

Jack laughed.

"Hey, why should the Naval Academy be any different from every other college and university?" Jack said, laughing

"I also get a lot of letters best described as 'whining.' " I said. "My predecessor encouraged anonymous messages directly from midshipmen to the superintendent, a stupid idea if you ask me. I get letters complaining about the course load, about the heavy physical fitness curriculum, and God knows what else. And these kids are here on the taxpayer's dime! Starting now, I'm going to drill these wimps like I drilled my pilots. Sorry I'm venting, Jack, but if I can't vent to you, who can I vent to?"

Jack smiled, winked, and squeezed my hand.

"Hey, Jack, let's talk about something more serious, at least more serious than some dickhead midshipman whining about having to do too many pushups."

"You mean the Greenbrier, Ashley?"

"Yeah, that's what I mean. Hell, it's been a month since we visited the place, and I'm still concerned about their lack of security. As brilliant a guy as Zeke Wellfleet is, he'd better get his act together about protecting that place. It's as if he never heard of terrorists. When I told him that the single word 'target' popped into my head when I looked at the Greenbrier, I meant it. From our little trip into the future, Jack, I know we agree that the Greenbrier and *The Keepers of Time* are critical institutions for the future of this country. I spoke to Bill Wellfleet two days ago. He says that Zeke's on top of it, but it's still only in early planning stages."

"Why don't we call Rick Bellamy? As head of Homeland Security, he may have some valuable tips." Jack said. "The Greenbrier is a private institution, but Rick has more ideas about fighting terror than the next 100 people in line. And he knows you and me."

As usual, Jack had a great idea. Unlike our new friend Zeke Wellfleet, I don't allow good ideas to percolate too long. There is a time for action and a time to think. It was time for action. I called Bellamy in Washington.

"Admiral Ashley," said Bellamy. "Congratulations on your new position at the Naval Academy. To what do I owe the pleasure of your call?"

"Rick, are we on a secure line?" I asked. "Jack's on speaker."

"Of course, Ashley. Fire away. Hello, Jack."

"Rick, you're aware of the Greenbrier Resort in West Virginia, I assume."

"Yes, it's a great place. I took a golf vacation there a few years ago. As I recall, it's also the place where the government was supposed to go in the event of a nuclear war. I believe it's now owned by some eccentric guy who uses it as a records depository of some sort. He may be eccentric, but he's onto a good idea."

"That's the place, Rick. To get right to the point, Jack and I have become friends with Zeke Wellfleet, the man you're talking about. Yes, he does have a good idea, and he's even formed an organization known as *The Keepers of Time.* Jack and I are convinced that he's running one of the most important institutions for the future of our country."

"Ashley, does this have something to do with that crazy time travel story about you and the *USS Ronald Reagan?*"

"Yes, it does, Rick, and when you have a few hours I'll tell you all about it. But for now, my major concern is that Wellfleet and his group need security. Yes, they're a private organization, but this issue involves Homeland Security. Rick, can you give me some ideas?"

"Jot this name and number down, Ashley—Angus MacPherson of MacPherson Security. He's a crusty old Scotsman and a brilliant businessman. He and I are good friends. I also have another name for you, a guy who you know well, Buster from the CIA. Because that Greenbrier outfit is private, Buster can't talk to you in an official capacity, but he has more ideas and cranks them out faster than anyone I've ever met."

"Rick, God bless you. I'm following up on your suggestions. Give our love to Ellen."

I looked at Jack. I took a deep breath and let it out. I was beginning to feel like something was happening.

"Hey, don't stop dialing now, babe," Jack said.

Looks like the Naval Academy will have to do without my services for a couple of days. I called Zeke at the Greenbrier to get a few meeting dates. Then I called Angus MacPherson at his New York Office.

"Hello, this is Admiral Ashley Patterson calling for Mr. MacPherson. Homeland Security Secretary Rick Bellamy suggested I call."

Nothing like dropping a big name to get your call answered. I explained to Mr. MacPherson, who did have a charming Scottish accent, that a company vital to the long range interests of the country is in a big need of security consulting. He told me that he was familiar with *The Keepers*, and that his company was a client. After checking with his secretary, he said the day after tomorrow would be fine. Then I called Buster.

"Ashley, how the hell are you? How's Jack?"

"He's on speaker, Buster."

"Hey, Jack," Buster said, "I don't know where I find the time, but I just read your latest book. Number one on the *Times* Best Seller List. Way to go, my friend. I loved the book and even took time to give it a five star review on Amazon. But I assume you guys didn't call to talk about books. What's up?"

I explained the Greenbrier to Buster, telling him that it was an important institution that preserved records. I didn't tell him about *The Keepers*, figuring that he'd find out all about them at the meeting. I told him that Rick Bellamy urged us to call him. Buster was fine with the day of the meeting. I also told him about Angus MacPherson, a man he apparently knew.

Jack and I met Buster and Angus MacPherson at the Greenbrier Valley Airport, just 20 minutes away from the Greenbrier Resort. Buster and MacPherson gave each other a bear hug. They were obviously old friends. When you know Rick Bellamy, your world gets smaller and your circle of contacts gets bigger.

We took a limo to the resort, and arrived at 11:30 a.m., just in time for Zeke to treat us to lunch in the private dining room. As we pulled up to the main entrance, Angus looked at Buster and said, "How difficult would it be to drive a truck through that door, Buster?"

"Truck?" Buster said, "How about a Volkswagen Beetle?"

When we walked into the main lobby, Angus turned to Jack and me and said. "We'll meet you in the dining room at noon. Buster and I would like to take a little walk around."

"Hey, Angus, why don't we walk through that door that's marked 'Vital Records?' " Buster said.

They walked through the unlocked door and saw the gigantic array of computers and electronic equipment. Every person they passed smiled and gave a cheery hello. They looked around to see if anyone was in uniform, such as a security guard. Nothing.

"A hot dog vendor on Lexington Avenue has more security than this place," Angus said.

After strolling around for a half hour, Angus and Buster joined us in the private dining room. Zeke and Bobbi, in their typical way, stood and smiled and gave a Greenbrier welcome to Angus and Buster. Bill and Magda Wellfleet were there too. Angus looked at Zeke, then at Bill Wellfleet.

"Are you two brothers?" he said.

"Long story, Angus, which we'll tell you about shortly."

As if they rehearsed the routine, Zeke and Bill walked to the front of the room.

"Between the two of us, we're going to tell you the story of the Greenbrier as well as *The Keepers of Time*," Zeke said. "First I'm going to ask Admiral Ashley and her husband Jack to talk a bit about time travel. I believe it will set the stage for everything else we're going to say."

Jack and I told them about the strange voyage of the *USS Ronald Reagan*, and eventually how we came upon the Greenbrier. If there's such a thing as a "skeptical expression," that was the face that Angus MacPherson wore. Buster, on the other hand, took it all in stride. He had time traveled with me and Jack back to World War II once. Long story. The point is—Buster gets it. Zeke then explained the story of *The Keepers*, past and present, and Bill told the saga of *The Keepers* of the future.

"Well done, Samah Zeke."

"Thanks, and you too, Samah Bill."

Angus and Buster just looked at each other.

We had lunch after Zeke and Bill's presentation, exchanging small talk, as if small talk were possible in a discussion of time travel and an averted nuclear war.

Zeke stood as coffee was being served.

"Now that we've given you folks an update on what this place is all about," Zeke said, "we can now get to our main topic of conversation—security. Angus, your comments, sir?"

"Well, lad, as you know, MacPherson International, including MacPherson Security, is a client of you *Keeper* folks. As a client, I suddenly find myself a wee bit nervous. When I'm asked to assess security for any kind of institution, it usually involves a massive amount of planning and money. But I don't think that will be the case here, you may be happy to know. The reason a security overhaul costs a lot of money is because we spend a huge amount of time and effort undoing things that were done wrong. That is not the case here—you have no security at all. We'll be starting from scratch, which is actually a lot easier than undoing bad procedures. You have absolutely no procedures. When Buster and I walked around before lunch, we did get a lot of pleasant greetings. But here we were, a couple of complete strangers, walking through a door that said 'Vital Records.' Nobody asked us to state our business. We also noticed that your main entranceway has nothing to block a vehicle from crashing through it. Zeke, lad, you have built a marvelous institution here. I find the mission of your organization to be inspiring. When Bill Wellfleet talked about the impact of *The Keepers* in the distant future—time travel skeptic that I am—I found myself thinking that this institution that's dedicated to preserving things, needs preserving itself. Zeke, I hope I haven't been too blunt with my assessment."

"Angus," Zeke said, "please don't apologize. Thanks to Bill Wellfleet, and now you, I'm convinced that I've been putting too much effort on our mission, and not enough time—not nearly enough time—protecting it. I'll openly admit that I haven't given it enough thought. My attitude has always been one of denial. I've always thought, 'Who would want to harm a harmless group like us?' Part of me still feels that way."

"I'd like to turn this over to Buster, our friend from the CIA," Angus said. "After what Buster has to say, you may discover that you have more enemies than you ever imagined."

Buster stood to address us. He's a tall, good looking guy with a swarthy complexion, a Middle Eastern appearance, and short-cropped black hair. He has broad shoulders and stands with the posture of a Marine. Buster knows how to talk to an audience as well as he knows how to interrogate a terrorist.

"As everybody knows, we recently averted a nuclear war," Buster said. "The major reason we were able to do that was Bill Wellfleet's convincing speech at the White House, not to mention the work of my good friend, Admiral Patterson. But make no mistake folks. As devastating as that war may have been, the reason it almost happened was because we were dealing with two weird messianic groups of people, the Iranians and the North Koreans. The idea of a nuclear conflagration suited them just fine, because they're not rational actors. Our enemy has changed, and it began to change way before the Iranian mullahs planned for the end of days."

"Buster, if I may," Zeke said, "just to keep us and especially me, focused, please define 'the enemy.' "

"Sure, Zeke, you bring up the most important point of all—know your enemy. Simply stated, our enemy is radical Islam. That shouldn't be a surprise. Going back decades to the massacre at the Munich Olympics, to the hijacking of the cruise ship, *Achille Lauro,* radical Islamists have hated us and wanted to kill us. 9/11 is the most dramatic example. We all know about terror. All you have to do is read the newspaper. But something has shifted in the past couple of years, something that, frankly, scares the shit out of us, pardon my Arabic. At the CIA we even have a name for our project, although, as a spook, I'm not going to go into much detail. Bill, I know you're from the future. Do you understand the word 'spook'?"

"Sure," Bill Wellfleet said. "A spook is a spy, a guy like you."

"Damn, you guys *are* good," Buster said. "The title for our project, and the name itself isn't Top Secret, is *The Shadows of Terror.* We call it that because our enemy has learned to lurk in the shadows. The typical suspect doesn't go to a mosque, may not wear a beard, never logs onto a radical website, and sure as hell doesn't look like me, with my Lebanese parentage. The terrorists we're seeing these days are 'home grown.' They may not even have a Middle Eastern background. They don't use Muslim names, but the names they grew up with here in the States. We're seeing fewer Ali Muhammeds and more Phil Smiths. We're also seeing Nancy Smiths. Let me give you a perfect example. I interrogated an attractive blond woman recently on suspicion of her being involved in a terror plot on a US Army base in Afghanistan. I won't give you her name, of course, but it sounds like the girl next door. She grew up in Iowa and is from Irish German heritage. As I look at Zeke's pretty fiancé Bobbi over there, I could swear that she was our suspect's twin."

"I don't have any sisters," Bobbi said softly, not attempting humor, just setting the record straight.

"So that is the new face of terror," Buster said, gesturing toward Bobbi. "Our suspect, who is now in prison, conspired to blow herself up with a bomb vest, along with a few hundred people in the middle of an Army hospital. She didn't have a hard time finding the uniform of an American Army nurse. She *was* an American Army nurse. That's what we're dealing with, folks."

The room got very quiet. Bobbi put her face in her hands.

"Any questions so far?" Buster said. "I hope you have answers, because I sure as hell don't."

"Buster," Zeke said. He wasn't speaking in his normally loud enthusiastic voice. His constant smile wasn't there either. Zeke looked troubled. "Do you have any specific suspicions about this place, the Greenbrier, any specific threats?"

"Nothing specific, Zeke," said Buster. "We have an inside mole, probably the most valuable insider we're ever had. I won't tell you his name or where he's from. All I can tell you is that his word is golden to us. He's never mentioned this place to me. This mole I'm talking about has an uncanny way of keeping his ear to the rail, and an amazing way of letting us know when something's coming. He tells us when he hears chatter in his mosque, or some random gossip in the street. He texts me every couple of days when he hears something interesting. I never heard of *The Keepers* or *The Keepers of Time* until you people told us about yourselves this morning."

Jack and I lingered over coffee with Bill and Magda Wellfleet while Zeke and Bobbi gave the full tour to Buster and Angus MacPherson. While we waited, we played Scrabble. Jack and I are good at Scrabble, well very good, actually. But we couldn't compete in the same league as Bill and Magda. Coming from 210 years into the future gives you a different perspective on things, I guess, including words.

The four returned to the dining room when they were done with their tour. Buster and Angus read from their notes about their security recommendations.

We had all planned to stay over that evening for a performance of *The King and I* at the Greenbrier's main theater. Jack and I planned to stay a couple of days more for some needed R&R. We loved the performance. Zeke invited us to join him and the cast for cocktails later that evening.

"Magda Wellfleet will soon take over as our new theater director" Zeke said.

"Two hundred and ten years from now," Ashley said, "as strange as that may sound, we saw Magda perform the lead in *The Sound of Music*. It's a memory that will never leave me."

The next morning we gathered in the private dining room for breakfast. Buster and Angus were waiting for a limo to take them back to the airport. We were still gushing about the performance the previous night.

Buster's phone buzzed. He excused himself and ducked out into the hallway.

When he returned to the room, his normally dark skinned complexion was white as snow.

"Holy shit," he said. "This is my guy, my main mole. I'm putting him on speaker. Go ahead, Mike. Repeat what you just told me."

Jack and I knew that Buster's "main mole" was Imam Mike from a mosque in Brooklyn. According to what Buster had told us, Mike is the most valuable insider the CIA ever had. He's a man who keeps his eyes and ears open for any hints of upcoming terror activities.

"The words of the week are," Imam Mike said over the speaker: "*The Keepers* and *The Keepers of Time*. I've heard these words constantly for the past three days. I had no idea what the words meant until Buster just told me. I understand that the *Keepers* organization is located where you guys are at the Greenbrier Resort in West

Virginia. Here's another word I heard a few times—bomb vests, that's *plural*, fucking bomb vests. Now get this, here's the other word I constantly heard—*Saturday*. Today's Thursday. I think somebody has plans for the Greenbrier in two days. Buster, if I were you, I'd get the fuck out of there."

"Mike, call me immediately if you hear anything new," Buster said. "Be safe, my friend."

Buster dropped his phone on the table, put his hands on his hips, and looked at us. Words weren't necessary beyond what Imam Mike just said. The Greenbrier is a target.

I looked at Angus.

"Zeke, we haven't made any formal business agreement yet, but a handshake will do fine. We need to staff up immediately. Metal detectors will have to wait for a short time. Figure a budget of about $2 million, maybe more, maybe less. Does that work for you?"

"Angus, please do what you need to do," Zeke said. "Whatever I need to budget I'll do it."

Angus took out his cell phone and dialed.

"George, it's Angus. Can you spare any guards from our project in Roanoke? It's about an hour and a half from here by car. Great, do it now, lad. Then I want you here tomorrow to supervise a staffing detail and lay out a plan for full security including metal detectors. Bring at least four men with you. "

He looked at Zeke. "How many entrances and exits to this place?"

"Four, including the main entrance."

"Make that eight men, George. See you tomorrow, lad."

"That was my chief of security," Angus said. "He makes things happen fast. Zeke, please tell me how many reservations you have for the next two days."

Bobbi got up and went to the front desk. She came back two minutes later.

"Two couples are checking in tonight, and six couples tomorrow," Bobbi said.

"As an innkeeper you won't like what I'm about to suggest," Angus said, "but you should contact those guests and tell them they can't come. Make up some kind of story about a gas leak or something."

"I'll handle it, Zeke," Bobbi said, as she walked quickly out of the room.

"How many guests are here now?" Angus said.

"Just about 300," Zeke said," including a Rotary group of 124."

"Can you give me their names and addresses in an electronic file?" said Buster.

"Sure, I can give them to you right now."

"Great, I'll run them through the CIA database to see if we have anybody on our watch list."

"What about the main entrance that you and Buster were worried about?" I said.

"Good point, Admiral Ashley," Angus said. "Zeke, do you have a truck that we can put in front of the main doors."

"Yes, it's our supply truck, about 40 feet long."

"Please have someone park it there now, lad," Angus said.

I leaned over to Jack. "Please tell me you have your service revolver, honey."

"Yes, you?"

"Of course."

Great, so at least Jack and I are armed, and I'm sure Buster and probably Angus. But now what?

━┼ ┼━

"Bring me up to date on our plans for West Virginia, Mustaffa," said Muhammed Sidduq. The two men sat on the open air terrace of a restaurant in Racca, Syria.

"Fifteen of our brothers are prepared to attack in two days, on Saturday, a busy day at the resort. All are armed with M16 automatic machine guns and 9mm Glock 17s. Each man carries two extra magazines. Five of the brothers will wear bomb vests, the newly designed ones that aren't too bulky and are less likely to arouse suspicion."

"But Saturday is June 21, the first day of summer, Mustaffa. How can someone conceal a bomb vest, even if it's a light one? The man won't be wearing heavy clothing."

"All of the brothers will wear loose-fitting Hawaiian style shirts. They conceal a lot."

"Are we certain there are no metal detectors at the resort?"

"Yes, Muhammed, we have checked it carefully. There is so little security it tells us that they never expect trouble of any sort. Seven of our men have already checked in."

Muhammed Sidduq laughed.

"Soon the infidels will have more trouble than they ever dreamed of."

━┼ ┼━

Buster walked back into the private dining room, which had turned into a command post, after a half hour of strolling through the crowds of guests.

"I was just looking to get some gut level impressions of the guests," Buster said. "One thing I did find strange, which leads me to a question. Is any group planning some sort of luau or Hawaiian celebration?"

"We have a Rotary convention starting this afternoon," said Bobbi. "I'll check with them to see if they're planning a Hawaiian party."

Buster paced in front of the room. I've known him long enough to see that something just popped into his mind. His facial expression made it obvious.

"Wait, wait, wait," Buster shouted, his hands raised. "This is bullshit. I don't know what we've been thinking. If there's an attack planned for Saturday, we don't know how many people will be involved, and from what Mike said, the event may include bomb vests. We need some heavy artillery. I gotta make a phone call."

Buster asked Zeke where he could find a soundproof office. Zeke showed him to the recording studio next to the main theater. About 25 minutes later Buster came back into the room.

"Our heavy artillery is on the way," Buster said. "I called Rick Bellamy, head of Homeland Security. When I gave him the specifics, especially the day, Saturday, he agreed to send in an FBI SWAT Team from the Washington office. Forty men will be arriving by helicopter this afternoon. I checked with Zeke, and the chopper will land in a field on the outskirts of the compound. If any jihadis are already on the premises, and I don't doubt they are, I don't want to raise any suspicions with a chopper landing in front of the place."

Buster wasn't exaggerating when he said "heavy artillery." SWAT stands for Special Weapons and Tactics. All major police departments as well as the 56 FBI field offices around the country have SWAT teams at their disposal. SWAT teams are used for high risk situations, such as hostage incidents. A SWAT team mission usually is more of a military type action than a typical law enforcement matter. If what Imam Mike said was accurate, the Greenbrier more than qualifies for a SWAT team operation. Buster arranged for an *Enhanced* FBI SWAT team, with a force of 40 officers and heavy duty weapons, including MP5/10 machine guns and M4 carbines. But how the hell can all that firepower handle a guy in a suicide vest? I wondered.

Lieutenant Mitchell Conklin, the commander of the SWAT Team, walked into our "command post" at 1400. Buster told us about the guy's background. He was a former Navy SEAL, and saw extensive action in both Afghanistan and Iraq. Conklin was 32-years old, medium height, about 5'10," and built like a wrestler. Zeke pointed me out to him, and he gave me a sharp salute, even though I wasn't in uniform. Buster introduced him.

"Good afternoon, folks," Conklin said. "Please pardon me if I'm blunt, but it's the only way I know how to act. We all know why my team is here, so I'm going to lay out our plan. I've conferred with Buster and Angus MacPherson, two men who know a lot about security. Here's what we're going to do. On Saturday morning, we're going to sound the fire alarm in all buildings on the complex. I've already arranged with the local fire department to have its trucks here to provide realism. I have two objectives—to save innocent lives and to kill our enemy. A few of my marksmen are already fanned out through the surrounding woods, with high-powered rifles. What can make this mission difficult is the intelligence that we have about suicide vests. We don't know how many there may be, but any number of bomb vests makes for a tricky situation. We can't simply shoot a guy we think may be wearing a vest, especially because we first have to identify him. If we shoot, chances are that he'll explode, and innocent lives may be in jeopardy. Suicide bomb vests have changed in the past few years. They're no longer as bulky as they once were, and don't need heavy clothing to conceal them, just loose fitting clothes. I'm curious, as we all are, about a group of men wearing baggy Hawaiian shirts. Because the temperature is warm, such a garment could be the choice for concealing a vest. I've seen a few incidents over the years of suicide bombers wearing exactly such clothes."

Bobbi raised her hand.

"I've checked with the Rotary group that's arriving this afternoon, and they told me that they're not planning any Hawaiian party. They also told me that 12 of their group are already here to set up the conference. We've checked them out, and they're all Rotarians."

"Thank you, Ms. Simmons," Conklin said. "That tells me that we have to look carefully at the group of men in Hawaiian shirts. It's possible that they're an advance team of jihadis. When the fire alarm sounds, we'll place smoke bombs near all elevators and hallways. It's non-toxic smoke, so don't worry. We just don't want anyone to think that the alarm is a drill. We want people out of the buildings. Some of my men will be will be in charge of moving the crowd of people. I don't want any Greenbrier personnel in uniform because they would make for ready targets. Our plan is to herd everybody into that large building that's used as for landscaping supplies. The building is being emptied of supplies as I speak to make room for everybody."

"Lieutenant Conklin," said Zeke. "Getting back to the bomb vests, will it be possible to pick out the suicide killers?"

"Once we get everybody out of the buildings and start to steer them to the landscaping building, we'll abandon our secrecy and my guys in protective combat gear will take over, including men in bomb-resistant clothing. We have bomb-sniffing dogs, but the jihadis will be aware of that."

"Do you expect that any of our guests will be injured, lieutenant?" Zeke said.

"I expect some of them will be killed," Conklin said. "Any other questions?"

CHAPTER FORTY TWO

I've been in situations when I knew my ship was in danger of being attacked. I've been aboard a ship when the attack actually happened. That's the deal with being in the military—it can get dangerous at times. But the expected raid on the Greenbrier was something new for me, actually new for everybody, except for the SWAT Team guys. It was 10 a.m. and the fire alarm would sound shortly. I'd be kidding you if I didn't say that I was scared. I was scared because we didn't know who the enemy was. We'd soon find out.

The show was about to begin. The alarm sounded, and Zeke announced over the intercom to all guest rooms that the building had to be evacuated. A lot of the guest spaces were ground level cottages, which made it easy for people to exit. Six employees were in charge of picking up elderly people and those with physical disabilities and taking them to the assembly building on golf carts. Jack and I walked to the assembly building, along with Zeke, Bobbi, and Bill and Magda Wellfleet. Buster had taken a position with the SWAT Team, along with Angus. The building was large enough to hold everybody. Problem is that the place stunk from the bags of fertilizer that had been removed the day before. I felt like I should be doing something more, but I realized that my job, along with everyone else, was to take orders from Lt. Conklin. He and his SWAT Team knew a hell of a lot more about such situations than the rest of us, myself included.

The SWAT Team, along with Greenbrier employees, guided the crowd across the lawn. On orders from Conklin, people were herded into small groups. If a bomb went off, or if somebody opened fire, smaller groups meant a margin of safety.

The SWAT Team knew what they were looking for—anyone dressed in such a way that could conceal a bomb, or a machine gun. A sudden gust of wind swept across the lawn. Conklin had hoped for this, because the weather reports called for a breezy day. Eight of the team were charged with keeping their guns on the six men in Hawaiian shirts. From my position, I could see three of them. Holy shit, I thought, as the wind blew the shirts tightly around the men. It was obvious that they were wearing heavy vests under the shirts.

"Execute," Conklin shouted into his radio. The SWAT Team sharpshooters opened up with their high powered rifles aimed at the heads of the Hawaiian shirt guys. Five of the men fell. The sixth man reached under his shirt. The explosion was deafening, and Jack and I hit the ground instinctively. I felt a piece of shrapnel graze my back, but the distance was enough to prevent me getting injured—or killed. I looked at Jack. He gave me a thumbs up sign. We both took out our guns.

The game was on, so it was no time to be timid. I saw a man in a raincoat running toward the center of the lawn. It's a sunny day, I thought. What's the raincoat all about? Jack apparently figured it out. As the man withdrew his automatic machine gun, Jack fired two shots to the guy's torso. He went down. Jack then fired a round at the man's head.

"Everybody stay down," Conklin shouted over a loudspeaker.

Anyone who was wearing loose clothing was a potential target, and the SWAT Team people knew that well. I was impressed with their discipline. They didn't just shoot at people in loose clothing. One by one, they would shout "freeze." Anyone who reached under his garments was killed.

Later, Bill and Magda Wellfleet told us about an incident in the landscaping building. Bobbi noticed a man in a flowing bathrobe. When he reached under it, Bobbi let go with a flying karate kick to the man's temple. He fell to the floor, and a SWAT Team member fired three shots, killing him.

The firing continued for five minutes. After the shooting stopped it was quiet, crazy quiet. We all knew that one or more jihadis could be biding his time, waiting for a target to appear. Ten minutes went by, with no more gunfire.

"Stay down," Conklin shouted. Smart guy, I thought. Never assume that a fire zone is clear until you're convinced. His men fanned out across the complex, looking for possible shooters. Another team inspected the bodies to report to Conklin.

After Conklin gave the all clear announcement, we gathered in the private dining room, the space we had used as our command post. The three Wellfleets and Bobbi were there, along with Angus and Buster.

Angus turned to Zeke and said, "I've always heard that the hospitality of the Greenbrier is legendary, lad. Thank you for a pleasant morning."

Although I couldn't believe I was doing it, I laughed.

Lt. Conklin walked in. He took a piece of paper from his pocket.

"I'm accustomed to people in a situation like this to want to hide under the table. I was amazed at the courage that all of you showed this morning. Hey, Lieutenant Thurber, nice shooting. Here are the results of this raid. Fifteen enemy dead, and only two guests, one of whom was killed by the bomb blast. We don't know if the other man was shot by jihadis or if he just got caught in the crossfire. I'm leaving behind 10 men from my team to make absolutely sure that the area is secure. Soon this place will be swarming with regular FBI agents. Be prepared to answer a lot of questions, over and over. It's been a pleasure knowing you folks. I think I'm going to bring my wife here soon for a golf vacation. I know it will be safe."

Zeke ordered trays of sandwiches for the private dining room, the place we'd be sequestered to wait for the FBI investigators.

Bill Wellfleet stood at the head of the room. We all sensed that he wanted to talk, so we gave him our attention.

"I know I'm speaking for Magda as well as myself when I say that I'm baffled by what happened here this morning. Yes, we've read about ISIS, al Qaeda, and the other denizens of radical Islam, but the senseless violence is overwhelming. In our time we had horrible killing, but at least there was a motive. It was either theft or sacrifice in the killing fields of the barbaric stadiums. Why would anybody want to attack a site like the Greenbrier? The attackers knew that they couldn't take over the place, not for long anyway, but yet they came here willing to kill and be killed for no apparent reason. Magda, your thoughts?"

Magda stood.

"Dahlings, after this morning I rather miss the folks from the Eastern Empire and the other barbaric towns. Yes, they were evil people, but their actions at least had a goal. As much as we study these radicals of Islam, we still can't understand their motives. Do they really think that God commands them to kill?"

Buster's phone rang.

"Pardon me, folks, I have to take this."

Buster left the room. The conversation continued about the non-stop violence of the 21st Century.

"I agree with Bill and Magda," Bobbi said. "As a journalist I've written countless pieces about radical Islam. But no matter how much I write, I still can't understand the motivations. They have nothing to negotiate. They just want to kill and die. They seem to be consumed by a hatred that we can't fathom. I'm stumped."

After 15 minutes, Buster walked back into the room. I've gotten to know Buster enough to tell when the pallor of his skin announced that there was a problem.

"I just got a conference call from my boss at CIA and our inside mole," Buster said after taking a deep breath. "Something big is up, something very big. I'm happy that today turned out a success, but as you know, the war is far from over. I have to grab my things. A helicopter will pick me up in 20 minutes."

"Is the problem near here?" I asked.

"You know I can't answer that, Admiral Ashley. You don't have a need to know. Actually, I don't think you want to know."

Buster walked out of the room.

"Ashley, Is this normal in 2018?" Bill Wellfleet asked.

"Welcome to civilization, my friend, welcome to civilization," I said.

CHARACTERS – *THE KEEPERS OF TIME*

Baxter, Max - Commander, Chief of Staff to Admiral Patterson
Bellows, Mark- General, Commandant of the Marine Corps
Billings, Joshua - Lieutenant, Army of the Eastern Empire
Blakely, Mike - Commander, Executive Officer of the *USS Ronald Reagan*
Bollard, Jane - Lt. Cdr. Communications Officer, *USS Ronald Reagan*
Borden, Hamlin - Leader of Buffalo Town
Buster - CIA Agent, super spy
Carlini, Bill - Director, CIA
Ciano, Dennis - Chief Master at Arms, *USS Ronald Reagan*
Clark, Tucker - Major, Commander of Marine Detachment, *USS Ronald Reagan*
Conklin, Mitchell - FBI SWAT Team leader
Cummings, Bill - Lieutenant, Deck Officer, *USS Ronald Reagan*
Drake, Adrien - Leader of Cleveland Town
Drummond, Wesley - psychologist and historian with *The Keepers*
Fornier, Madelaine - Linguist with *The Keepers*

Goodkind, Jerome - General, United States Army Chief of Staff
Greenstone, Walter - Oceanographer
Jackson, Randy - Chief of Staff to President Reynolds
Johnston, Joseph - Commander, Navigator, *USS Ronald Reagan*
Jorolomen, Robert - Leader, Hollywood Town
Lang, Jeremy - Leader, Miami Town
MacPherson, Angus - Security company owner
McCracken, Randolph - General, Chairman Joint Chiefs of Staff
McGrath, Simon - Leader of Pittsburgh Town
Molloy, George - Medical Officer, *USS Ronald Reagan*
Monkton, Edward - Scout for *The Keepers*
Monkton, Margaret - Scout for *The Keepers*. Edward's wife.
Parker, Muriel - Commander, Engineering Officer, *USS Ronald Reagan*
Patterson, Ashley - Admiral, Commander Carrier Strike Group 2311
Patton, Jake - Marine platoon leader
Phillips, Lysle - Air Wing Commander, *USS Ronald Reagan*
Reynolds, William - President of the United States
Shaffer, William - Lieutenant and metallurgist
Simmons, Roberta - Reporter, *The New York Times*
Thurber, Jack - Writer, lieutenant, Ashley Patterson's husband.
Tomlinson, Harry - Commanding Officer, *USS Ronald Reagan*
Townsend, Roland - Admiral, Chief of Naval Operations
Watson, Sarah - Director, FBI
Wellfleet, Bill - Leader of *The Keepers of Time*
Wellfleet, Ezekiel - Founder, *The Keepers of Time*
Wellfleet, Magda - Theater director, actress, and Bill's wife

ABOUT THE AUTHOR

Russ Moran is the author of *The Gray Ship* (Coddington Press, 2013), Book One of *The Time Magnet* series. It's a story of time travel, romance, and a nuclear warship that finds itself in the Civil War. *The Thanksgiving Gang* is the sequel, *A Time of Fear* is Book Three, *The Skies of Time* is Book Four in the series, and The Keepers of Time is Book Five.

The Scent of Revenge, is the second book in the Patterns Series, the sequel to *The Shadows of Terror.*

The book you have just read, *The Keepers of Time*, is Book Five in the *Time Magnet Series.*

Russ Moran has also published five nonfiction books: *Justice in America: How it Works—How it Fails* (Coddington Press, 2011); *The APT Principle: The Business Plan That You Carry in Your Head* (Coddington Press, 2012); *Boating Basics: The Boattalk Book of Boating Tips* (Coddington Press, 2013); *If You're Injured: A Consumer Guide to Personal Injury Law* (Coddington Press, 2013); *How to Create More Time* (Coddington Press, 2014). He's a lawyer and a veteran of the

United States Navy. He lives on Long Island, New York, with his wife, Lynda.

If you enjoyed *The Keepers of Time*, please consider leaving a review on amazon.com.

To make sure you don't miss out on Russ Moran's forthcoming books, visit his website, http://www.morancom.com, and click on the "subscribe and get updates button."

THE BOOKS OF
RUSSELL F. MORAN

The Gray Ship – Book One of *The Time Magnet Series*
http://amzn.to/16GPumH

> "This provocative, intensely powerful novel is a must-read
> for sci-fi fans and Civil War aficionados, though main-
> stream fiction readers will find it heart-rending and inspir-
> ing as well. A rare read that's not only wildly entertaining,
> but also profoundly moving."

> — Kirkus Reviews

The Thanksgiving Gang – Book Two of *The Time Magnet Series* http://
amzn.to/1NzBs7N

> "I had never read a book before written in an efficient,
> minimalistic prose... Instead of writing what most readers
> want to read, he gives voice to life-like characters, with their
> flaws and prejudices. They are not infallible superheroes.

It's always nice to find a new voice in fiction and to enjoy creativity at its best."

— C. Ludewig

A Time of Fear – Book Three of *The Time Magnet Series*
http://amzn.to/1zdjaG9

"His story is fascinating, and adds even more depth to this already cavernously deep novel. Amazingly unique, chilling and well written, Moran weaves a future that is both desperate and hopeful. Blending modern fears with science fiction results in a tale that will keep you reading long into the night. Five stars!"

—Heather

The Skies of Time – Book Four of *The Time Magnet Series*
http://amzn.to/1CCC3jg

In *The Skies of Time*, you will recognize the two main characters, Ashley Patterson, now an admiral, and her husband, Jack Thurber. They met and fell in love in *The Gray Ship*, and now they're in for the adventure of their lives in *The Skies of Time*. Ashley and Jack have been such prominent characters in all four books of The Time Magnet Series that I feel like they're old friends. You will also recognize some of the other characters. But if I told you who they are, it would ruin the fun.

The Skies of Time is a novel of time travel and alternate history. Naturally, the book is fiction, but I've tried to make it as realistic as possible. Ashley and Jack are faced with the big question that troubles all time travelers—dare they change history? As the author, I'm the last one to be a spoiler, so I'll leave the answer to the characters in the book.

"I'm big fan of this series and this one may be the best. I hope there is another book to this series since it keeps getting better. There is a few questions I have about certain events that makes the next one even more suspenseful. These are great books to binge read one after the other."

— Time Travel Fan

The Keepers of Time – The book you have just read, is Book Five of The Time Magnet Series. The further adventures of Admiral Ashley Patterson and her husband, Jack Thurber. "A wild time travel tale, 200 years into the future—a new world, a scary world."

The Shadows of Terror – Book One of the *Patterns Series*
http://amzn.to/1IDQzJS

A novel that explodes off the front page of your newspaper.

Terrorism now has a new face, a face that's obscured in the shadows. The radical forces of destruction have learned to make themselves invisible to the West, and preventing a terrorist attack has become almost impossible.

A new war has begun, World War III.

Rick Bellamy, an FBI agent who specializes in counterterrorism, is engaged in his own war, a war with no end.

Bellamy's wife, Ellen, a prominent architect, discovers that she's in the middle of the greatest terror plot to date.

To defeat the enemy, Bellamy first has to uncover the clues, to shine a light on the shadows. He has to find patterns – before it's too late.

> "Move over James Patterson and Mary Higgins Clark. There's a new guy in town. Russ Moran's new book – *The Shadows of Terror.*"

> — Frank from Lynbrook

The Scent of Revenge, - Book Two in the *Patterns Series.*
http://amzn.to/1UvDRmw

The world is at war – World War III. FBI Agent Rick Bellamy and his wife, Ellen, find themselves in the middle of a sinister terror plot.

Someone is attacking young prominent women, inflicting a horrible disease.

Nobody knows its origin, nobody knows how to stop it, nobody knows how to cure it.

Rick Bellamy and a team of scientists want to go on offense. But how?

Will the lives of the women be changed forever? When will the attacks stop?

> "Heart pounding, can't put down thriller that will force you to look at terrorism in different light. Life in America will never be the same."

> —Cold Coffee Cafe

Sideswiped - Book One in the Matt Blake series of legal thrillers.
http://amzn.to/1MkxX35

Trial lawyer Matt Blake took on a perfect case.

It involved a sideswipe collision in which his client's husband, an investigative reporter, was killed. The evidence of negligence was overwhelming. Eyewitnesses testified that defendant was talking on his cell phone when he hit the other car.

But was it negligence? Was it an accident?

Or was it murder?

Matt uncovers evidence that the act may have been intentional. Somebody wanted the man dead. Somebody wanted the man silenced.

Somebody had a lot to hide.

The signs started to point to the highest levels of government.

An open-and-shut personal injury case suddenly became a vast conspiracy of terror.

"This books hooks you in from the very first line. You are drawn into the world of Matt Blake and become emotionally attached to him and his journey. The story itself is so well-written and moves quickly so there is never a dull moment."

—Sarah Elle

The Reformers is Book Two of the Matt Blake series of legal thrillers, the sequel to *Sideswiped*.

To be alerted to my future novels, please go to www.morancom. com.

Russ Moran

Made in the USA
Columbia, SC
24 October 2020